THE LAUGHING GIRL

by

Peggy O'More

Author of "LESSON IN LOVE" *and* "NONI"

Sherry Sadler, a newcomer at Avondale High School, had had enough ups and downs in her short life to take both good fortune and bad luck with equanimity and to laugh away minor worries. When a trip to the supermarket, in which she spent the last of her mother's hard-earned money for groceries, ended in a fall and a batch of broken eggs, Sherry took the incident in good spirits and was thankful that it gave her a chance to meet some of her new classmates.

Her attitude puzzled Judy Scotts, a "poor litle rich girl" who found it difficult to make friends, and antagonized Mona Delane, a serious-minded student who, in order to have a cause, invented crises where none existed. But Geary Cleveland, Mona's co-worker, was attracted by the new girl's infectious gaiety.

THE LAUGHING GIRL

THE LAUGHING GIRL

by

PEGGY O'MORE

Alouette Romance

By

Sharon Publications, Inc.
Closter, NJ

Copyright © MCMLXIII by Arcadia House
Published by
Sharon Publications Inc.
Closter, N.J. 07624
Printed in the U.S.A.
Cover illustrations by Kim Mulkey
ISBN 0-89531-143-7

THE LAUGHING GIRL

1

If I hurry, Sherry informed her mirror, I'll have time to swing around by Avondale High just as the kids are coming out.

She'd look over those she passed, and maybe, just maybe, one would smile or speak or even walk with her. That would be a real icebreaker. She'd start school on Monday, knowing someone.

Life was really super. Imagine two schools within one year, like two big buffets from which to make a choice of friends. There wasn't anything she enjoyed more than people.

Not even clothes, she thought, slipping into a wide, bell-top coat of creamy tan and settling a matching hat on hair nearly the same shade.

And then her laugh rippled out. The coat had been

given her mother to cut into strips and braid into a rug she'd been making.

Well, they had cut one strip. She was wearing it on her head, pleated, and it looked like a million.

A quick glance around the apartment. Her mother would find order when she came in from her first day on a new job. And weren't they lucky to have found such a place at such a price!

Not a real apartment, she conceded, hurrying out a private doorway. Just an old house converted, but we have the first floor wing. And there's a view, and above all a hallway, so if I and my friends make too much noise it won't bother the adults.

She'd better run along and look over her future friends, then go on to the shopping center and put on a demonstration of "how to buy food for two meals with almost no money." Her mother had been too excited to ask how much she had left.

Tuna puffs, decided Sherry. Half a dozen eggs and a can of tuna; two for the puffs leaves two each for breakfast. Coffee and milk and bread and—whoops!

She skidded on ice. She, who'd been ready to limit her clothes to sun suits and bikinis when she'd heard they were moving to California.

Her mother had waved a map before her, showing her the state ran more north and south than east and west. They were not going to the highly advertised section of palm trees and sun-baked beaches.

Ah, there was Avondale High School. It looked like California, long and low, with a red tiled roof and creamy walls. And she was too late. Students were pouring out of doors and down streets like creeks heading for a main river.

Lake, she corrected herself three blocks away. For here was a big shopping center with simply everything, and she'd swear the only kids not swirling around in the center had been carted off in school busses.

Up a ramp, down which buggies of groceries were delivered to cars, and into the supermarket.

Stop thinking about kids and start thinking about what, if anything, we brought with us.

Milk and bread, coffee, fruit juice (a sale on big cans). Maybe a small box of pancake flour, shortening of some kind. Tomorrow night they'd really stock up; they would have the car. Tonight, what could they do without?

And of course, after her mother's first pay check, they'd go all-out on an emergency shelf.

That was the fun of having had grim times; good times made you feel so rich. She kept an anxious eye on the checker and the amount he was totaling up relentlessly.

Whew, she breathed in relief. She had exactly enough, right down to the penny.

The big bag was awkward, so she carried the carton with its half-dozen eggs in one hand, paused at the door to look out. The lights had come on, and the square looked like a circus or a fair. The malt shop next door simply bulged with Avondale students.

That one boy leaning against the building—was he ever moody, shoulders hunched, hands thrust deep into his pockets! Oh, no wonder. He'd pulled one hand up to push back too long, lank hair. Even with the cuffs turned down, his sleeves didn't come near his wrists.

He'd be good-looking if he didn't look so angry.

Now down the ramp, then a diagonal cut across the square, and she'd stop and look at the fruit stand.

She didn't. One moment she was walking along. The next one foot went east, another west, and she due south, with a most peculiar thump echoed by cans rolling out of a broken bag.

"Are you all right?" asked an anxious masculine

voice.

She was, except for the darkness.

"Don't move," ordered a feminine voice, and a thin hand clamped down on her shoulder.

"She's wearing her hat on her face," observed a third voice thoughtfully. "Here. Oh, hello."

The third voice, or second girl, had removed her hat and Sherry, bewildered, looked up into grey eyes. Then she looked at the anxious voice. He had the most wonderful blue eyes she'd ever seen.

"Witnesses," the second voice belonging to the hand holding her down was making a declamation. "We need witnesses."

Sherry looked around. What else did they have? To her it looked as though everybody in the square were either crowded around or peering over the crowd.

"She should sue," the second voice was announcing. "Pure carelessness on the part of the market. As long as they get their money first, they don't care what happens to the customer. Now don't move; you are hurt."

"Oh, but I'm not," protested Sherry, trying to squirm out from under the firm hand. "When I felt myself going, I made like a rubber band."

"As in football," approved Blue Eyes.

"You don't play football on cement," stated she of the firm hand.

Sherry squirmed uncomfortably. She would that she *had* sat on cement.

"Please," she bubbled, "I didn't slip. Some small boy darted in front of me, dragging a stick. It caught me between the ankles; see where it snagged my stocking? I went down smack on half a dozen eggs. The thick carton broke my fall."

"And that," said Grey Eyes, "wasn't all that was broken."

"Oh, dear." Sherry put down a hand and lifted it quickly. "No eggs, and my last penny *kaput*."

"Young lady," a new voice had been added, a man's voice, and she felt two strong hands lifting her, "I am the store manager. It will be my pleasure to replace the eggs and the hose."

"You hear?" cried firm hand triumphantly. "Bribery."

"No, a pleasure," reiterated the manager, "to find someone honest and not out to get something for nothing. Jack," he called, "paper towels on the double."

"And a new bag for her groceries," advised Grey Eyes. "I'll convoy her home, if she'll accept."

"Will you, Judy?" asked Blue Eyes. "We're due at a committee meeting."

"Wait," ordered Judy, and surprisingly, even those not interested did. "I think introductions are in order. I'm Judy Scotts. This," she indicated Blue Eyes, "is Geary Cleveland, known these days as Dreary. And this," she yanked the girl of the firm hand center front, "is Mona Delane. You're new here, aren't you?" she asked Sherry.

"Mother and I arrived late yesterday. I start at Avondale High on Monday. I'm Sherry Sadler."

Sherry, now fairly well rubbed off by paper towels, was told to wait. She was willing but preferred backing up to a building.

She heard Judy sing out, "Hi, Jerry," saw she was backed beside the boy in the shabby clothes and smiled at him.

"Boy, you sure made a mess of your coat. But," he shrugged, "gives you an excuse to get a new one."

Sherry laughed. "Excuses I have; money I haven't."

"Then whatcha laughin' about?"

"Me," she replied. "You've heard about breaking ice at parties; the get-acquainted bit. Well, today I set out hoping to break Avondale High ice. Instead I broke eggs."

When he smiled he looked like a different person. "I'd say you broke ice as well as eggs. Look at the friends you made. What I don't get is giving up a chance of real money for eggs."

Sherry fitted her hat to her head, thankful it had been rescued. "Oh, that. I'd have had to lie. Lies are like rotten eggs. They look all right from the outside, but break one open, and phew! Imagine having to live with the odor; it would take all the fun out of the money."

"How come you know all that?"

She had promised her mother she would draw a blind on the past, but sometimes it slipped up a little and memory returned. There was a vision of a gracious home, her mother, still white-lipped from the shock of her father's death, and then the people who had come in with lies.

A hidden clause in a contract, and there was no home to sell; no money from that home to see them through their period of adjustment to a new life.

"Give," ordered Jerry.

They'd stopped at their old home town en route west. They had visited next door to their home. They had left, pitying those who had stolen from them.

"Oh," the blind was down again, "I watched some people living with lies they'd told for money. They were miserable. Here's Judy," she ended in relief.

And here were Judy, the store manager, and behind him a car attendant, all laden. Judy, she supposed, had had shopping to do.

Judy's car was a modest, dark blue affair. Sherry slid into the seat, the coat with its stains folded up away from the upholstery.

Then, after gay goodbyes, they were on their way.

"That boy I was talking to," Sherry pompted, "looks so unhappy. I think he'd be nice and good-looking if he weren't so angry at the world."

"Jerry Pedlar," Judy replied soberly. "I know. His people were transients, and I can't get to him to explain all people were at one time. Only the early settlers were called adventurers and pioneers. He worries me."

"Oh?" But Sherry made it a question.

"He's getting in with a no-good crowd. They call themselves a club, The Defiants. But it's not a club; it's an outright gang. They defy anyone to catch them destroying property.

"Half Jerry's trouble is his clothes. Being a boy is

rugged. Girls can make things over, but boys—"

Sherry frowned. "You don't mean Avondale judges kids by their clothes?"

"Anything but. Some of the kids come in looking like they'd rolled through a rag bag and worn what stuck to them. But you see, they know they don't have to wear such things. Jerry knows he hasn't anything else.

"Then there are some kids from the migrant camp who don't have good clothes, but they're so interested in other things they don't worry. If Jer would just let me talk to him—"

"Why not?"

Judy turned a distressed look upon Sherry. "You'll learn. You don't know about me. When you learn, you probably won't want to be friends, either."

Sherry hid her dismay. She liked Judy. What on earth could be wrong with her or her family to cast such a shadow?

2

They had drawn up before the entrance to the Sadlers' apartment, but Sherry sat still. "How about briefing me?" she suggested. "You'll tell me the truth."

Judy nodded. "I have a big, beautiful home with acres of garden. Gardening is Mother's hobby. And," her voice lowered, "a private swimming pool."

Sherry waited a moment, but nothing more was forthcoming. "And none of the kids ice skate?" she asked.

Judy gave a sharp laugh. "You would," she protested. "And no, it isn't steam-heated. It's just—well, we're the only ones who do have."

"My," Sherry said gloomily, "being different sure does carry a penalty. I doubt if it will affect me or my feeling. Mother and I have had everything from our own swimming pool to state welfare. Come to think of it, we really appreciated the welfare checks more than the pool. We could eat with those."

Judy looked at her, found her laughing and laughed with her. "We'd better get your groceries in if you're to have dinner ready for your mother."

Sherry said she could carry the bag and the eggs. From now on she'd be on the lookout for small boys. But when she picked up the packages she noticed Judy gathering other bags.

"But—" she began to protest.

"Stop quibbling. This is the store manager's thank-you for restoring his faith in people. I told him you'd meant you hadn't more money with you; not that you had actually spent your last cent.

"I also told him," Judy sighed, "you'd just arrived from the Midwest last night."

Sherry clung to the eggs. She'd almost dropped them. How on earth had Judy known from what section of the country they'd moved?

In the kitchen, Sherry began sputtering as Judy unloaded bags. "We used to have a Welcome to Our Town deal," Judy explained. "Whenever anyone moved in, the merchants' club sent a hostess with baskets of local produce. This is the same idea. Mr. Martin is glad to have people like the Sadlers here."

"All I have to say," Sherry finally managed, "is why doesn't our government employ women in their diplomatic corps? War would become as archaic as dodo birds."

They made a tour of the apartment, in order but not pretty as it would be within twenty-four hours.

"We carry our own drapes and knit slip covers," she told Judy, "window curtains and bedspreads. In no time we feel at home wherever we are. But I didn't have time to press them today."

"It would be fun to help," Judy said wistfully.

"As ironing isn't my favorite sport," Sherry admitted, "why not come and talk to me while I work?"

She would. She'd be there at nine o'clock, then stay for lunch to meet Sherry's mother. They'd have a ball, a real ball.

After Judy had driven away, Sherry started dinner, puzzled. Now why should Judy, a native of the town, have neither duties nor dates for Saturday? Duties, she supposed, were cared for by servants, but how about girl friends, to say nothing of boy friends?

Mrs. Sadler came in just as Sherry was ready to fold

the stiffly beaten egg whites into the tuna and rice crisp mixture. She flopped into a chair, pushed her hat back and looked around.

"You miracle," she said. "This order and food, too? I almost stopped to shop, but I was too bushed."

"Wait till you've enough oomph to look on the shelves." She dropped a spoonful of the mixture into the hot oil, then turned at her mother's cry.

"Sherry, what on earth happened? You didn't charge, did you? I'm sure you couldn't have had much cash left."

"Nu-uh." Sherry returned to drop more of the mixture and spoke above the sizzle. "I sat on half a dozen eggs, and they hatched. Mums, go get comfortable, I can't leave these now, and I can't give a blow by blow account without gestures."

By the time Sherry had the tuna puffs stacked like so many golden balls on a hot platter, Mrs. Sadler returned. She looked refreshed, relaxed and, of course, beautiful in an attractive velveteen muumuu that had once been somebody's raincoat.

"Now tell me," she ordered.

Sherry made her report, forgetting nothing, and Mrs. Sadler laughed.

"Isn't this wonderful?" she asked. "I didn't tell you I was worried for fear you'd have some extra need for cash at school and we'd have to decide which was more important: food or else. The mill pays only twice a month."

"Good; if it paid every week we might go overboard four times a month."

"Now tell me about this Judy. Has she another name?"

"Umhum, Scotts. Mother, what's wrong?"

"Wrong? Nothing. Oh, it couldn't be. I mean that's not an unusual name. Did you say Scott or Scotts?"

"What difference would it make?"

"Actually none, but there is a Scotts who is a heavy stockholder at the mill. Immensely wealthy, I understand. Oh, but if this girl asked to help you with the ironing—"

"Meaning you never lifted an iron in your balmy days?"

Sherry allowed herself to worry all through the drying of dishes. Her mother had never been the least conscious of the "haths and the hath nots." Having experienced both, she insisted she could see no difference.

No, there was more than Judy had revealed in her

brief confession; something that made her shy and un-sure of being welcomed.

She remembered now how the others had treated Judy. Mona had acted superior, yet she had obeyed. Jerry had looked at her as though he hated her. The store manager had treated her with deference. And Geary?

"Well," she conceded, "I wouldn't want him to treat me that way, as though I belonged to a different species of the human race."

Later she asked, "Would you rather I didn't make a real friend of Judy if she is your Mr. Scotts' daughter?"

"Whatever gave you that idea?" Mrs. Sadler re-proved her. "You know how I feel about your friends; I care about character rather than social or financial standing."

"Then why did you say she couldn't be your stock-holder's daughter?"

"Oh, that." Mrs. Sadler dried her hands and reached for the lotion bottle. "She'd be attending a private school."

Her mother having retired early, Sherry went to the tiny sunroom converted into a bedroom for herself to sit watching moonshot clouds trying to erase the stars.

Tomorrow she'd have a wonderful time. She'd learn about Avondale, the teachers, which ones Judy liked and which ones to approach on tiptoe. And the kids, especially, she admitted to herself, Geary.

She supposed Mona was his steady date. Too bad. Judy had said, when she'd introduced them, "known these days as Dreary." Why?

Judy was there bright and early and eventually got around to answering the question.

"He used to be fun. Then he got to running around with Mona and became 'a man with a cause,' all hepped on rescuing the downtrodden."

"Oh, dear." Sherry shuddered. "Mums and I had a couple of those working on us one time. We didn't know we were 'poor things' until they elected us to be their cause.

"Maybe we didn't have sense enough to mourn the loss of money; we were having such fun trying to pull two ends together to see if they'd meet."

Judy held up a curtain she'd just ironed. "I know. Mother and Dad were married during the depression. She says they had a wonderful time. She still cans everything we grow on the place as though another crisis were about to arrive.

"Dad says he's going broke replacing the jars she has to give away because we can't use half of it."

The ruffled kitchen curtains were put up and they stood off to admire them. Then Sherry brought the conversation back to Geary; she was blessed if she'd call him Dreary.

"I suppose Mona's his steady date for dances and things."

"Ha. Mona doesn't dance or go to any school affairs except lectures."

"A potatoes and gravy with no dessert girl," decided Sherry. "I like cake and pie and ice cream after a long stretch of steady study."

Judy sank into a chair, looking somber. "There are those who won't accept it. Then they get mad and go out to hurt the ones who have it."

She was speaking of the gang, The Defiants, Sherry knew. And now Judy was looking up at her earnestly.

"I just have to talk to someone about Jerry. Why do I have to like him better than anyone I've ever known? He could be so wonderful, but now he's letting his studies slip and—"

She hesitated, and Sherry waited.

"There's this gang. They're going to get into trouble, get caught. They're so no-good they'll see that Jerry's the one blamed, and once a boy has a bad record it stays with him.

"Sherry, I can't reach him. He hates me. If you really truly haven't any money, he'll like you. Will you help him?"

3

Sherry's reply startled Judy.

"No," she said; then her laugh rippled out. "I'm not a Mona. Maybe that's why he's defiant. He's tired of being helped. Being helped sort of means being looked down on, doesn't it?"

"You mean people shouldn't help others?" protested Judy.

"Nu-uh. Grab the other end of this drape, will you?" She knew what she meant, but she didn't know how to explain to Judy. "I mean being helped to help yourself is okay, but taking things people give you to make themselves feel big and superior makes you feel weak when you need to feel strong."

Judy argued. Sherry said nothing; each drape she hung made the living room more beautiful. She and her mother had achieved these drapes by doing without other, less important things. Sacrifice, some called it. Perhaps that was why they seemed so wonderful.

Why, it was almost worth becoming a "cause" if she could inveigle Dreary into visiting her and seeing these.

"They certainly do something for this room," Judy interrupted herself to remark, "bring sunshine into a north room. And your slip covers match the dull green of the leaves."

"And," added Sherry, twinkling, "we did them ourselves. I mean we saved the money and bought the drapery material. We'd have made the slip covers, too, but we moved so often we couldn't match the shape of what lay ahead."

She could laugh about it. They need not have moved. They were eligible for different types of pensions—veterans', for one. But her mother didn't like to be limited; she accepted what they needed with gratitude, then studied to fit herself to earn more.

"And so you see," Judy went on, "that's why teen-agers have so many stories told on them. It's their parents' fault, their neglect, their—"

Sherry's smile checked her. "You say Jerry has a fine mind. Okay, a fine mind will get around to figuring out the backgrounds of our most famous men. Some were reared in luxury, given the best education. Others pulled themselves up by their bootstraps. Fifty-fifty. It's whats inside that counts. If Jerry has it, he'll make the grade."

Sherry had lunch ready when her mother came in at one o'clock. Judy was to tell her parents later it was not what she'd prepared but what she'd made of it, and the way it was served.

What she made of it, she repeated to herself, remembering their conversation.

She had asked if there wasn't some way she could help Jerry, and Sherry had replied, "I think so. Stop pitying him. Believe me, when you're down, nothing eats into your morale like pity. Makes you want to do something bold to show off how smart you are."

At the moment Sherry was pitying herself. Here she was with a brand-new friend, a senior when she was only a junior, and her mother wasn't the least enthusiastic about her friendship.

"But why, Mums?" she pleaded. "She's a lovely girl, and lonesome for some reason. She said her mother would call, and we'd be invited out for dinner."

Mrs. Sadler groaned. "That's it, dear. I'm new on a

position very important to us both. If we accept such an invitation, the people at the mill will feel I am trying to secure my job socially rather than by efficiency. Your Judy *is* the daughter of our Mr. Scotts."

For a few moments Sherry sat frowning; then she laughed. "Am I ever glad we're poor. But nobody can be afraid to be friends with me. Maybe that's why Judy's lonesome."

The apartment and their clothes for the next week being in order, Mrs. Sadler decided they should spend Sunday afternoon becoming acquainted with the town.

It lay north and south, strung out along a main highway for blocks, though only four blocks deep. And it had, Sherry thought happily, everything anyone could want.

Near sunset they drove west on a county road to search for the river, finding it high with rains, trees which would shade summer picnic spots up to their branches in brown water.

Imagine—river and mountains and Avondale High School. And Dreary.

Perhaps, she reasoned, she should have felt strange about starting at a new school the next morning. But walking along, looking at students zoom by in cars or trot or teeter or stride, she didn't.

People, she reasoned, were like flavors: some sweet, some sour, some spicy, and some she'd rather not taste. But she had a choice, and what might be good for her wasn't for another.

Having a choice was a privilege, she thought, and then drew her shoulders together defensively. A sharp voice had sounded behind her; a firm hand gripped her arm. Here I go again, she sighed inwardly. Choice my eye.

"Sherry, how do you feel? Are you all right? Are you sure you feel all right?"

She had until then and said so.

"I'll take you in to Professor Cartwright," stated Mona Delane, and into Professor Cartwright she took her, talking steadily. Sherry cast wistful glances at students who watched from the sidelines.

Mona literally overrode the office attendants, hand still firmly on Sherry's arm, until they faced the principal.

"This," she announced, pushing Sherry forward, "is Sherry Sadler. She had a dreadful experience Saturday."

She ranted on, repeating the charges Sherry had heard, until Cartwright stood up.

"Mona, classes will be called within a few moments. If you will leave, please—"

She had a last few words on the way out, and Sherry couldn't help smiling. Short of thrusting her out physically, which would be against the law, the head of the high school couldn't win until Mona was ready.

"Now," he glanced down at papers on his desk, "Sherry, about this accident. Should you wait a few days before entering?"

"No, sir, I wasn't hurt. I used to ice skate and know how to fall. Besides," a tiny laugh escaped, "I landed on an egg carton."

"I see. Would you like to give me your version?" He made it a demand, and Sherry didn't know he wasn't interested in the fall but in the perspective of this new student.

He was wiping his eyes when she finished. "Then, short of being baffled by sudden darkness, you suffered no injury and actually came out the winner."

"Yes, sir. Mr. Cartwright, why do people laugh when they fall and others laugh when they watch?"

"Some psychiatrists say it is a hold-over from learning to walk. We don't remember, but after we learned to take a few steps, to toddle, we usually sat down hard and unexpectedly. Our first impulse was to cry. Parents, or whoever was watching, laughed, and soon we laughed with them."

"A fun thing." Sherry nodded.

"That was how you met Mona?" he asked.

Sherry's shoulders showed inside laughter. "Yes, sir," she replied, but her eyes told him she knew she had become a cause. "And several others," she added.

He had studied the papers her mother had left at the school and doubted she would have any difficulty in adjusting to the slightly different curriculum. In some studies she would be ahead of the class; in others, behind. From her record he was confident she could equalize the two.

She was then turned over to an assistant to choose her electives and to pay her registration fee, then taken to meet her advisor, Mrs. Hanson.

"And now, Sherry," said Mrs. Hanson, after a few moments spent discussing the school she had left and the one she was entering, "it is our policy to place students new to the town with some friend, or to appoint a student to assist them through the first few days."

The person appointed would take them to classrooms, to any scheduled sports or social events, introduce them to other students.

"Mona Delane," said Mrs. Hanson, "has asked for the privilege of—" She stopped at Sherry's sharp indrawn breath. "You have met her?" she asked. "You are friends, are you not?"

"I talked to her Saturday a few moments. This morning she steered me to the principal's office."

"Steered," said Mrs. Hanson, and smiled.

"Wouldn't it be all right if I just sort of barged around and got into wrong classrooms?" Sherry asked anxiously. "What Mother calls the trial and error method?"

"For you, yes; for the other students you might create confusion."

"I wouldn't want to hurt her," Sherry began. "If you've already told her—"

"No," Mrs. Hanson said. "I suggested she was carrying too heavy a load of outside activity. Ah." She had run a slim finger down a list of names, and there was nothing in her expression to indicate she had been evaluating Sherry before deciding upon her school escort.

She left the small glassed-in office to go into the

library where students were either studying, doing re-search or serving as librarians.

Anxiously Sherry watched. Mrs. Hanson had stopped at the main desk, and now a girl turned toward her, and Sherry could tell by the way she acted she was pleased by something Mrs. Hanson was saying.

Tall, slim, she was trying to smooth a tousled mass of light brown curls as she followed the advisor.

"Sherry, this is Catherine, who will help you for a few days, Miss Sadler, Miss Cleveland."

Cleveland. She couldn't believe it, but looking at the girl, she knew this was Dreary's sister.

"I know all about you," Catherine confided happily, when they reached the hall. "Geary came home Friday simply raving. He said you were one wonderful brick, the way you laughed about what happened to you."

"I felt silly," Sherry insisted. "You try sitting on eggs. Now had I landed on flowers or something lush, I might have pulled a swoon."

"Mona told me she was taking you over this morn-ing," Catherine went on as they reached the locker room.

"Mrs. Hanson thought she carried too much work already," Sherry faithfully repeated the advisor's words.

"Does she ever! And if you ask me, Geary's the reason. Honestly, there are times when I could wring his neck. He could be such a nice guy again, but he's gone all out to save the world."

"Meaning it doesn't need saving?"

Catherine stopped to look at her searchingly, then, seeing the dancing light in her eyes, laughed.

"Dad says it wouldn't if people had sense enough to learn how before they went into action. Oh oh, look who's here."

"Oh, there you are." Mona stalked in on her thin ankles. "I've looked everywhere. I am to introduce you around Avondale."

"Mrs. Hanson says I'm to," Catherine objected stubbornly. They were off in a word battle, with Sherry standing by, longing for a carton of eggs to sink onto. Anything to get out of her role of a bone fought over by two angry beings.

4

Mrs. Isabel Hanson, alerted to an impending battle in the locker room, stopped just outside the door as a high, clear laugh rang out.

"You're wonderful, both of you," Sherry said, "and I don't know why I'm so important to either one."

"Well, I do," flashed Mona. "You are new. You need to get in with the right students. Catherine hasn't a serious bone in her head."

"Unlike some, I have no bones where they should not be. Nor has Sherry."

"She's furious because I've helped Geary recognize his debt to society. And what's more—"

Again Sherry's laugh checked her. "Goodness, Avondale is different from any school I've ever attended. I would have supposed the advisor made the decisions.

Mrs. Hanson has appointed Catherine. Shouldn't you discuss this with her, Mona?"

Mrs. Hanson beat a quick retreat, but not to her office. Mona's favorite class would be called within a few minutes. She would cool off before the two were free again.

Mona made one scathing remark about a newcomer daring to criticize a school she knew nothing about and departed.

"If you ask me," Catherine said soberly, "she is afraid of you. Any time Geary shows any interest in any girl, she latches onto her, then needles them in front of him and the other kids until they show up foolish."

"That's kind of pathetic," Sherry returned. "When kids or people needle others, it's usually because they're not sure of themselves inside. Well, what's next?"

By the time Catherine had taken her over the school, the nine-forty buzzer had sounded. They had a ten-minute break, and Catherine made the most of it, introducing her to so many students she knew she'd never remember any of them.

Judy passed with several girls, slowed and stopped to speak, then went on.

"I didn't know you knew *her*," Catherine said accusingly.

"Judy was part of my audience Saturday," Sherry reminded her. "Then she drove me home and—"

"Of course." Catherine brightened. "I remember Geary saying so. She's okay, but the only kids who go with her are ones whose parents have an axe to grind."

"Translate," suggested Sherry.

"Well, I mean kids whose folks work for Scotts or want something out of him, like backing or trade or just being able to say they know him real well."

Sherry shook her head. "That must be rugged, never knowing you could be liked for yourself."

"I never thought of that. Maybe that's why she acts so dopey sometimes."

The buzzer stopped further conversation, and Sherry went to her first elective. She'd had typing one and two and was ready for advanced shorthand as well. She had decided (because her mother had had no business training at the time of her father's death) the quickest way to help with the family finances was to take basics of a business course.

She wouldn't participate that first day, so she had time to wonder. Why was Judy treated as she was at

Avondale? Sherry's grandfather had been quite wealthy at one time. She was positive her mother hadn't faced such a problem. Yet look at the way she'd acted about the Scotts.

Crazy, she decided, and looked up to find a girl staring at her with hostile eyes.

She was overdressed, wore too much makeup, and her hair was bleached. Methodically Sherry reviewed the outside, then sought the reason she had made an enemy of a girl she'd never before seen.

She described her to Catherine as a "pretty blonde who seemed to have something against me."

"Oh, her." Catherine literally tossed her over her shoulder. "That's Jammy. Her name's Jamaica, for some reason, but everyone, even the teachers, call her Jammy. She's a transient."

"So am I," laughed Sherry.

"You're different. You wouldn't get in with a gang and hang around showing off. She's way out on a kid named Jerry."

"Jerry Pedlar? He was in on my big crash. We talked a little."

"So you have the answer. He doesn't like girls. If he talked to you and she saw you, look out."

Finally she had to ask what Sherry was laughing about.

"Seems I broke more than eggs on my crash. I fractured friendly relations." Silently she listed Mona, Judy and Jerry. She hoped there were no more.

Her next period, English Four, she considered not friendly relations but finances. Avondale had no school cafeteria. It had the actual rooms set aside and equipped, but Catherine had explained they had had to close down.

"Too many of the kids come from farms. They'd rather go down to one of the cafés on the main drag and pay more for less. Worst of it is: those who don't live close enough to go home for lunch have to do the same or look like squares."

Eight blocks home, eight back. At least seventy-five cents a day for lunch, or being considered a square because she carried hers. Five school days. Wow! Fifteen dollars a month?

She could do what Catherine reported others did: bring sandwiches in a sack, then go to the malt shop and have her sandwiches there. And she needn't always buy a malt; if she hadn't the cash a coke would give her the right to eat with the gang.

It was quite a problem, especially in a new school. Well, thank goodness she had enough cash to take care of the first day.

At the Malt Shop she found there was still another solution to lunch.

Catherine had met her at the room door. "Come on," she urged; "we'll have to run for it. The girls have gone on to save us a seat, but—"

And they ran for the three blocks, pushed through a crowd waiting outside, through a second one inside, and finally, with cries of triumph, slid into a booth made for four but now holding six.

"I'm splurging today," Catherine informed the rest of them. "Give me the ninety-cent dinner, and then I'll order dessert. What's for you, Sherry?"

Sherry settled for a schoolburger, wondering what it was but content with the fifty-cent price.

"Cathy's showing off," one of the girls said. "She can save her lunch money. She was smart; she hooked Larry."

"Larry," another offered, "has a car and lives in her neighborhood, so they breeze home for lunch."

"Oh, well, you'll be lunching with us from now on," one said confidently.

"No," Sherry objected, "I can't afford it."

In the next booth there was a sudden silence, then scuffling, and the waitress saying sharply, "Boys, you know the rules."

Under cover of their argument Sherry went on, "I mean I can think of other ways I'd rather spend the money. I guess," she looked ruefully funny, "I'll have to date material in my end of town."

They laughed and happily began checking possibilities but not really finding any.

"Geary would have been a bet," Catherine said. "I mean he wouldn't have minded swinging around that way. But since Mona's come into his life they have deep, dark committee meetings at the oddest hours."

Sherry enjoyed the chatter, especially about Geary. She felt she knew him better with every word.

She also enjoyed the schoolburger. Not much meat, but enough melted cheese for protein, and such a walloping slice of onion she felt it alone would waft her to school.

A few times she looked around, but the café in self defense had relegated school service to a back room with high-backed booths, and she couldn't see much.

"Mostly juniors here," the girls reported. "Seniors go to a real swank spot up the street; sophs have a counter deal; and most of the freshmen carry their own until they're hep."

"I can't see Mona at a swank spot," Sherry said thoughtfully.

"Rather not. She carries her own. Gives her a chance to lecture the unfortunates, as she calls them."

Oh, dear, thought Sherry, Mona's lectures she could do without. On the other hand, if she could watch Geary they might be worth it.

The first day of school over, she started home briskly enough, began to lag by the sixth block and by the eighth felt herself really dragging. But then she always felt that way her first day at a new school.

Swiftly she changed to a housedress, made up beds left to air that morning, made the cup cakes and, while they were baking, set the breakfast dishes to soak.

As the cupcakes cooled for icing she washed the dishes, swept, then began thinking of the next day.

Carrot sticks. Should I wear the same dress? I could put dip in those little maraschino glasses I saved. Wonder why I didn't even see Geary today. Maybe mother would like that little thermos of juice instead of coffee. Hope it doesn't rain; I haven't a decent water-shedder for my head."

She iced the cakes, thinking of the teachers and kids; which ones she felt were friendly and which ones were going to require digging down to know.

When the rap came at the door, she jumped and dropped a cake, icing side down, naturally, then spun around to find Jerry staring through the pane at her.

"Come in, Jerry," she called.

"Gee, I'm sorry."

"Serves me right for being jumpy. Here, have one. They're good."

My, how he stiffened as he said, "No, thanks."

"Don't trust my cooking, or what? You act just like Mums and me when we were having a tough time. We would sit and drool sooner than accept any—"

"I'll take the one that dropped," he barked.

"Okay, the floor's clean. But aren't people funny, Jerry? When they know they can buy things for themselves, they can accept gifts and love them. When they can't— My, were we ever dopey! Here, have some milk. And if you don't eat a really good one, I'll never talk to you again."

Jerry shook his head." You're the craziest," he said. "Oh, I came about the morning paper. Kid brother has this route, and I thought maybe your mother would like a subscription. Folks who lived here did."

"We'd like it, but not yet."

He frowned, started to rise, then sat back. "Gosh, Sherry, you shouldn't go around telling things like that. It's all right with me. But at the Malt Shop, you saying you couldn't afford to buy your lunch could give people wrong ideas, kids and grown-ups too."

Sherry sat up, alert. Jerry had been one of the boys in the booth next to her.

"I tried to cover for you, but the guys heard you."

He'd started a row and been called down by the waitress—for her. Now what should she do? If she explained, he'd feel worse than ever.

"That was gallant," she managed, wondering where the word had come from.

Gallant. Why, he looked better already. Maybe it was the cup cakes, but she didn't think so. Could be he had not had many real compliments, and one made him feel worthwhile.

A tap sounded at the hall door, and there stood the landlady, Mrs. Malthropp, looking grim.

"Oh, brother," muttered Jerry. "Be seeing you." And he fled out the other way.

5

"Sherry," Mrs. Malthropp began talking the moment the door opened, "I promised your mother I would keep an eye on you. I do not think it advisable for you to entertain friends here alone."

"Oh, Jerry just came to see about us taking the morning paper. I'd just iced the cup cakes and wanted him to have one. Do try them."

"Don't care if I do." The big woman sank into a chair and reached. "That boy," she sighed, "and that boy's family."

"Give them a hand and they bite it. I'm surprised he'd accepted a cup cake. I've cooked big meals, all the things I thought a boy would enjoy. He'd put in a good morning's work for me. I knew he was hungry, but would he eat? No."

"I guess his shame at being hungry was bigger than the hunger," murmured Sherry.

"Should be; not that it's his fault. Like all transients, the moment they get their hands on cold cash they put on a show, if it takes their last cent."

Sherry's eyes were dancing. She remembered the first time her mother had had a little extra cash. Instead of buying something sensible like groceries, she had taken Sherry to a store where both bought completely silly play shoes they didn't need.

"It makes them feel rich," she sought to explain. "People need that sometimes, don't they?"

Mrs. Malthropp sighed deeply and launched into the story of Jerry and his family.

The Pedlars had come to Avondale four years before, destitute. They'd found a small cottage on the edge of town and various organizations had given them enough "cast off" furniture to make it habitable. Relief agencies had seen they were fed, provided with fuel.

"That next year and the one after they worked like Trojans," Mrs. Malthropp said; "field work, any kind. The mother canned everything she could find for winter. The father spent his time off helping woodcutters and taking fuel wood in exchange.

"They made enough to buy the cottage, a tag end of an estate no one had wanted. The executors were anxious to close out. Mrs. Pedlar had a green thumb, and by the next spring the place looked like a picture postcard.

"Well, sir, they had a chance to sell at a good profit. They did. Junked their old rattletrap car and bought a shining big new one—that is, made a down payment—then took off for their old home across the continent to show folks how rich they'd become.

"Not a lick of work did a one of them do last summer, as they were visiting kinfolk. They come home when school started, rented a cheap place, and right away the car was repossessed.

"They've had a grim time, and what's worse, they won't let nobody help them. Who's that out there?" she broke off to ask.

Sherry looked out. A white-blonde head was moving behind a bank of shrubbery. Waiting for Jerry? He'd slipped out the other way.

"Oh, dear," cried Sherry. "Mrs. Malthropp, would you mind walking to the door with me? I think that's a girl who's clear gone on Jerry. I don't want her to hate me."

Mrs. Malthropp did more. Sherry found her a mistress of intrigue. She said all of the right things, then ended up, "Now don't worry about that morning paper subscription Jerry was trying to sell you. You come along in with me and get mine. Got some magazines for your mother, too. Then we'll have a spot of chocolate."

From a rear window they watched the white head move across the lawn through the dusk, stop before windows, then scurry back to the street and head for town.

"I do declare," sighed Mrs. Malthropp, "you youngsters have a harder time than grown-ups."

"How?" Sherry asked earnestly.

"You don't know the time will come when you can look back and laugh at your troubles."

Oh, but she did; she just hadn't applied that knowledge to her current affairs.

"I'd better hurry," she said. "Mother will be in within half an hour."

She was, and found a tasty dinner awaiting. When she had finished, the dishes had been put away and Sherry was bringing out her homework, she asked a question her daughter was dreading.

"And now tell me what you are worrying about."

Sherry explained the matter of lunches.

"I've been listing costs, Mother. I know I am eligible for a letter man's sweater. I've had ice and roller-skating and swimming and tennis and all that sort of thing."

"Well?"

"There goes the first twenty-five dollars. Then a junior class pin will cost another twenty-five. Then there are all of the little things that will add up unless I deliberately go out for a boy friend to pay for them for me, and I can't do that.

"There are tickets to out of town games and, unless I find a date with a car, transportation on the school bus. School plays and buying project things like candy and cookies and stuff. And class fees and—"

"How about basic costs?"

"Pencils and pens and notebooks and paper and—"

"Now tell me what this has to do with lunches."

"I study better if I've had a decent lunch. Lunches would run at least fifteen dollars a month. If I carry my own, I'm a square. What should I do?"

"Are you a square? Then why not set a precedent?

Laugh. Carry your lunch and have so much fun a lot of girls who haven't the nerve to be different will start carrying theirs. Just one rule—"

"Don't alibi?" asked Sherry, and her mother nodded.

Sherry started for school the next morning carrying a lunch box. It was enameled to match her school coat, and in big contrasting letters was printed: "MY LUNCH."

Jerry was the first to see it. Sherry would have sworn he turned pea-green.

Judy was next. "Sherry, you're wonderful," she cried. "I envy you. That place where I lunch covers a dab of nothing with mashed potatoes and toast."

"Be my guest."

"I wouldn't dare," Judy replied unhappily. "There'd be a run on the bank and foreclosures in all directions if I did something that looked like economizing."

Catherine came swinging up, saw the lunch box and laughed. "I have to hand it to you, Sherry. If it wasn't for that noon bit with Larry I'd join you. But, sweetie, look out for Mona."

She didn't look fast enough. Mona saw her in the locker room and nodded gravely. "It is well to admit one's place," she said. "Of course you will join us?"

"Sorry; not this time." Sherry had her answer down pat from much mental rehearsing. "Change in schools. I have to catch up on two subjects. I'll be studying."

The lunch box had a greater effect upon Mrs. Hanson than on anyone. She had gone on to her first class, just off the library, dazed.

A nonconformist, she mused. So is Mona. I wonder what impact she will have on morale.

There had been a time when Sherry might have worried about doing things differently, but now that she had tasted responsibility she thought more of preparing herself to be a wage earner than as the leader in a popularity poll.

As the noon hour approached she squirmed a little. It would be fun to go to town with the girls, a real break in her serious studying. And she could. She had money in her pocket.

And I want to keep on having small change there, she stated to herself, waved the other girls on and, after picking up her lunch box from the locker room, sought the lunch room.

It was a room which would seat three hundred. Fortunately, it had an ell, and this was screened off for the few carrying their lunches; some fifty, Sherry thought. In other words, one hundred eyes were watching her.

She walked to the unoccupied end of the room, spread her lunch on a napkin, then, book propped up against her lunch box, tried her mother's exercise of tuning out everything else.

It couldn't be done. Mona came in with Geary, and while she might have tuned out Mona, Geary she had to watch.

He'd be wonderful if he laughed, she thought, but he looked so horribly earnest.

They sat at the head of a long table, and Sherry would have sworn the kids all squirmed.

"Perfectly ridiculous," Mona was saying. "Here we have this big, perfectly equipped cafeteria, and the school board hasn't sense enough to insist it be used.

"We should have balanced meals served here—"

"Gee, Mona," rasped one boy, "they'd cost something. Maybe not as much as in town but—"

"For boys like you, Teddy, there would be no cost. Only the ones who could afford—"

"You mean charity?" a thin voice asked. "We'd be set aside, sort of?"

"No one but the board members would know."

"We'd know," Teddy informed her. "That's okay for little grade school kids, but school boards talk. Me, I'd rather eat hay."

"You shouldn't feel that way, Ted." Geary spoke for the first time. "Our nation needs strong minds. Strong minds come from strong bodies."

"The heck they do," Ted blustered. "How about Einstein?"

"Nevertheless," stated Mona, "we intend to take action. We shall go from door to door with a petition. Each of you will canvass your area or one to which you will be appointed. You must forget your own personal desires and think of the greatest good for the greatest number."

Geary shifted uncomfortably, and Sherry switched her gaze from Mona to him. There; he'd seen her. She smiled, and he smiled back, and Mona snapped:

"Geary, the petitions. Distribute them."

He didn't do a very good job. Short of a fire drill, Sherry had never seen a room empty so rapidly. She would bet there would be a lot of hungry kids in afternoon classes, unless they had sandwiches they could cram in their pockets.

It was Isabel Hanson's day to stand watch, as the

teachers called the noon duty.

She wished there were some law she could impose which would bar Mona Delane from the lunch room. There was none, not even a law which could silence her. She doubted that existed any place outside the library.

Ah, now Geary and Mona were approaching Sherry. She wondered how the new girl would react. She was looking up, laughing.

Sherry couldn't help laughing. Mona reminded her of a goose they'd had, Esmeralda, who was forever strutting around and calling attention to herself.

"Hi," she greeted Geary, and literally swam in the smile he returned.

"Well, give her a petition and tell her what to do," ordered Mona.

6

Sherry was still laughing, but now there was a slight contempt in her eyes. She couldn't like a boy, no matter what kind of eyes he had, if he jumped to a Mona's command.

"No point," he said to Mona, but looked at Sherry. "She's new here."

"I'm quite sure," Mona informed him, "she would prefer a decent lunch to being half starved and trying to maintain her grades."

"Mona!" Geary swung on her.

From her eyrie Mrs. Hanson started forward, then stopped. Sherry was laughing aloud, a beautiful, contagious laugh.

"Half starved?" she said after a moment. "You insult my cooking. I really prefer it to food cooked in the mass. Here, try a cup cake."

Geary looked down, saw there were two and smiled again. "Um, good," he said after a bite.

"Geary," Mona again, "do come on." And now she was indulgent. "We really can't expect a newcomer, especially someone from out of state, to take our problems seriously."

"Wait, Geary flung back, and studied Sherry. "Which would you rather do: bring your lunch, eat downtown or have the school cafeteria open?"

Sherry braced herself. Laughter came to her aide. Those two looked as though the fate of nations hung on her words.

"For goodness sake," she said, "why are you two all steamed up about the cafeteria? Frankly, I'd rather have freedom of choice.

"And if I have to carry my lunch, I'd rather not be made to feel I'm sitting on a street corner with a tin cup held out to catch a stray dime."

"Come on, Geary." Mona's voice was lofty. "She knows nothing of the hunger of those who were here. She's never suffered."

"Mona means—" Geary frowned—"some of those kids come from the migrant labor camp."

"So their parents are eligible for surplus food. You know," Sherry's head tipped and her eyes asked Geary to share her fun, "the best thing that ever happened to us was being hungry.

"As long as we were well fed we sat around like two fat slugs, moping. Then when rations got scarce we got the lead out of our shoes and began working to see it wouldn't happen again.

"That's the wonder of being an American. You have a choice, if you don't mind working."

"Geary," there was a snap to Mona's voice, "we have a committee meeting. You may not remember you are chairman."

Geary nodded at Sherry, smiled and gave her the okay sign. "Be seeing you," he said, and it was a promise.

Sherry turned back to clear away her lunch and return to studying. She was so happy she thought she just might burst and litter up the room. Geary wasn't a square; just an eager beaver trying to do something someone had sold him on as being right.

Mrs. Hanson, literally mopping her brow, also turned back to her lunch and a book. She didn't read. She talked to herself.

Amazing. Had the new girl been angry her argument wouldn't have touched Geary. Laughter had such a curative quality.

Sherry didn't accomplish much as far as study was concerned. A few had remained in the lunch room. One had scurried out and returned with Teddy in tow, and Teddy stalked up, looking angry.

"So you think it's smart to stand in line and wait to have someone hand you out surplus food."

Sherry looked up. Teddy reminded her of Jerry. She bet this was the younger brother, the one who had the morning paper route.

"I didn't say that. I said it was lucky to have food when it was needed. Believe me, I know. And I said I was glad I'd been through it. I am. It gave us the oomph to pitch in and work for the kind of food we preferred. Everybody has to work to achieve."

"Who's kiddin'? I know folks who don't lift a hand and get everything laid right in their laps. I know a girl—"

Quickly Sherry stopped him from mentioning Judy's name. "Big houses, lots of food and good clothes aren't fun when you're suffering from another kind of poverty.

"Nothing's worse than loneliness, lack of friends, people misjudging you because they can't see you for the things you have that they want and aren't willing to work for. I can't think of anything as poor as someone without real friends."

"Aw, salami. You talk hash."

"Bless you." Sherry was laughing again. "I think I can stretch day before yesterday's meat if I add something. Now I know what's for dinner. Hash."

"She's nuts," Ted informed the listeners. "Come on; maybe we can grab a coke before class."

But Mrs. Hanson had seen his face. He was disturbed. He'd had some of his pet hatreds struck a telling blow.

Sherry was puzzled when, during afternoon study break, she was surrounded by girls; first Catherine and her friends, then others.

She, they informed her, had stood up to Mona.

"Nu-uh," she objected. "I only stood up for myself. Don't you?"

The answers came. "Easier to keep out of her way." And "She can out-talk any of us." And "Listen to her, and the first thing you know you're stuck with some committee duty."

Later she watched a strange pantomime and wondered about it. Judy came out for a touch of winter sunshine, alone and looking so lonely, with everyone else in groups.

Then two boys broke away from a crowd. Jerry and Teddy went over to her and the three walked away for privacy, then stood talking earnestly.

When Judy returned, alone, her expression was puzzling to Sherry. She looked happy and completely bewildered.

Judy caught her just after the last class. "Sherry, something wonderful happened. May I drive you home?"

"And me wondering if my puppies would carry me that far. I'd love it, Judy, if you don't mind swinging by the market. I'm not buying eggs."

The market was a friendly place. Mrs. Sadler had shopped there on Saturday afternoon and thanked the store manager; now Sherry was gently teased.

"We could stop for a malt or something," Judy offered as Sherry returned to the car. But Sherry knew Judy was more interested in telling her some secret than in drinking malts or anything else.

"I'll make chocolate at home," she said.

The moment they were under way Judy started. "Sherry, the very most wonderful thing happened. I'll burst if I don't tell someone who won't tell anyone else.

"You know the Pedlars rent from us. Dad has an old house on the flats he'd planned to tear down. Well, then Jack Pedlar came to see if they could rent it. No one in town would rent to them.

"So Dad said okay. He didn't want to charge them anything, but neither did he want them to feel beholden, so he made the rent fifteen a month.

"They couldn't even pay that. He didn't care, but they did, and that's one reason Jerry hates me so.

"Well, today Teddy and Jerry asked me if they could do some work around our place to pay for their rent. Isn't that purely wonderful? I mean, they can stop hating us."

"My, yes. And you do have work."

Judy almost stopped the car. "Oh, Sherry, we really haven't a thing. Dad has so many helping out. Ooooh," she wailed, "what am I going to do?"

"Think," Sherry suggested.

"Think?" squealed Judy. "What good will that do?"

"It works." Sherry was laughing. "If I hadn't stopped

moaning and started thinking the time I fell in the well when I was a kid, I wouldn't be here now."

"I'm in a well. How did you think your way out?"

"There was a ladder just out of reach. I thought if the crazy kids at the top would stop yelling and start pulling on the rope, they could pull me up far enough for me to grab it."

Judy thought all of the time Sherry was preparing hot chocolate; then Sherry had an idea.

"Why did your Dad want the place torn down?"

"It's such an eyesore. We look down on it from a terrace."

A moment later she cried, "I have it. Dad can let them work out their rent by fixing it up. Oh, no, that won't do."

"Why not?"

"Because he plans to get rid of it as soon as the Pedlars move. That would make them feel worse than ever, as though their work weren't good enough to keep."

"You're right. Well, keep thinking while I make the beds. Nothing Mother dislikes more than coming home to unmade ones. Won't take a minute; we both sleep easy."

She had her mother's half made when she went skidding into the kitchen. "Judy, is it a big house? Well, when we were driving west we were held up because some cottages were being moved."

"Oh, wonderful. Dad has all kinds of equipment on call."

"Keep thinking."

Her mother's room in order, Sherry dashed into the sun room, then started laughing.

Judy joined her. "What is it?"

"Look at that tree with its hair all tangled up in clouds. Can't get loose."

"Sherry, you're the craziest. But it really is. Hasn't it sense enough to know those clouds will turn to rain in no time?"

"Well?" Sherry turned to her.

"Oh, so I stop tangling my brains with clouds and wait. Sherry, this is the prettiest spread. Bet you made it."

"You know my stitches?" She looked down at the crinkle crepe with its salmon pink roses, the wide flounce of eyelet embroidery that had once decorated a costume her mother had worn to a ball.

"No, the colors; your toss pillows of salmon pink

and green and white. It looks—well, happy."

"Why not? It's cheered some pretty drab rooms."

Judy turned suddenly. "Sherry, I have the solution. You will come home with me for the weekend, won't you, and help me put it over with Dad? Mother plans to call Saturday afternoon and invite you folks for Sunday dinner, anyway."

Sherry was hearing her mother's groan when she had identified the Scotts. She'd foretold this. Now how, oh how, was she going to get out of it without hurting Judy?

7

Sherry collapsed into a pint-sized rocker and began to laugh. "It's all so silly," she began. "No, not your invitation; just things."

"Things?"

"You know that girl, Minerva something? The one who more than topped everyone else at Avondale in study rating?"

"Rather. No credit to her; she's Cartwright's niece."

"You mean each teacher graded her with one eye on pleasing Cartwright? Nu-uh. I think she's a brain. Must be rugged on her. She can't help being smart, but she'll never get any credit."

"Sherry, I can't see what this has to do with you spending the week-end with me."

"Suppose this was a business instead of a school, and

Minerva were working, supporting a family. Would the students or fellow workers give her credit for being good, or would they say her uncle gave her top pay because she was his niece?"

The brightness had left Judy's face; the sullenness was returning. "I suppose you mean your mother is working for some outfit in which my father's interested."

"She is. What's more, she borrowed money for specialized training. She just has to show the manager and her co-workers she's efficient so she can hold that job."

"But Dad would—"

"Oh, Judy, don't you understand? Getting along with the people you work with is most of the battle. If you don't, your work is ten times as hard. It's funny but it's true.

"And it won't be forever, just until she proves she's capable. Besides, if I were with you, your Dad might think I dreamed up the Pedlar deal."

Judy lifted her head. "The same thing, isn't it? He wouldn't believe his youngest had brains enough to think things through. Why," her face was brightening, "it *is* silly." And she joined in Sherry's laughter.

"It doesn't mean you and I can't be friends," Sherry insisted.

"Oh, look." Judy pointed to the window. "The elm is rid of her clouds. I'd better hurry home; that is a real storm blowing up."

At the doorway, she turned. "Sherry, you don't know how much being friends with you means to me. Half the time I think kids or their parents have an axe to grind with Dad, and I'm ashamed to think that way."

"With me," Sherry laughed, "you know I'm trying to keep the axe away from the grindstone."

She hurried then, chopping celery and carrots, a hand full of nuts, what was left of the meat and potatoes, then shaping them into patties.

Time for a cake or cookies; she'd given away more of last night's cup cakes than she'd eaten.

Mrs. Sadler literally swam in. "My, what a storm!" she said happily. "And what smells so good? I'm starved. How did your day go?"

Sherry gave a humorous account, and Mrs. Sadler laughed right up to the Judy episode. "You didn't have to hurt her?" she asked. "I'd rather be called a sycophant than that. I've learned quite a bit about the Scotts since we talked."

She told Sherry about it later. Mr. Scotts had come to that area as manager of the very mill in which she was working, many years before. Because he had foresight, he had analyzed business trends, bought small holdings which prospered, retained his interest in them even after he had gone into business for himself.

"And people resented his success, even those his money helped ride the post-war adjustment period."

"Why?" asked Sherry.

"I suppose they were jealous. He worked and studied and used good judgment, where they had tried to conduct business as usual, refusing to face a change; perhaps too indifferent to make the effort."

It was right he should have a beautiful home; he did a great deal of entertaining of out of state business men. This, too, the town resented.

His two older girls were married before the silent feud against him reached its peak. Judy, ten years younger, was the one to catch the impact.

"Why didn't he send her to a private school and save her from misery?"

"As it was told to me, he knew, as you and I learned, even a great deal of money can vanish rapidly. He wanted her to learn how to get along with all types of girls and boys."

Dishes done, they sat before the fire listening to the rush and roar of the storm.

"Mother," Sherry said earnestly, "please don't become too successful. Living like this is so cozy."

"Oh, get on with your homework." Mrs. Sadler laughed. "And, dear, it isn't the size or beauty of a home that counts; it's—"

"I know; what's inside that counts. Now to American problems."

But when she started studying she wondered if what she had participated in during her off school hours hadn't been one of the greatest of American problems: adapting to others who represented many different financial standings, none of them realizing his was a classification which need not be permanent.

The storm blew out during the night, bringing a dawn so perfect Sherry felt she had to wear something to match it.

That blue suit, with a blouse as fluffy as the white clouds racing across the horizon, trying to catch up with the storm that had left them behind.

As she dressed, Sherry thought of the suit. It was an old one of her mother's. She had ripped it to pieces, then had turned it, steamed and pressed the cloth. Her mother had re-cut it to modern lines. Sherry had basted it, and Mrs. Sadler done the final stitching.

Walking to school, she thought of the hours she had spent on the suit. Maybe she'd given up some fun with the other kids, but it was worth it.

If there was only some way to make over shoes, she thought as she came to a small lake. Leaves and debris had blocked the sewer inlet, and between her and the crossing was a great sheet of water. She needed boots to navigate it.

A car swished past, slowed and backed up. Then cautiously it drew up to the curb.

"Want to try my pontoon?" asked Geary Cleveland.

"Do I ever!" breathed Sherry. "I thought I'd have to build a bridge." And she slid into the seat beside him.

"My, you look fresh," he said, sending the car ahead. "Hey, I didn't mean you look fresh; I mean—"

Sherry's head tipped back. "I had that coming," she insisted, laughing. "It was such a gorgeous morning I tried to match it. I think it's fun matching clothes to weather."

"Must take a bankroll to do that."

"No, imagination and a good needle hand."

"How about a dark, cloudy day with a mean wind? Do you look gloomy and try to freeze people?"

"That's when I forget people with my color hair aren't supposed to wear red. No, I defy those days."

In the next block she asked, "How did your petitions come out? Did many sign?"

"Came to a grinding stop, that project. Guess we didn't think it through before we launched it. School wouldn't have closed the cafeteria before a pretty thorough investigation. But it sounded good."

Fortunately they drew up to the school parking lot, for Sherry didn't know what kind of a comment to make. Nor would she have had time for anything lengthy. Mona was bearing down on them.

"Thanks for the rescue, Sir Walter Raleigh," Sherry said, and slipped away from the approaching menace.

Judy signaled her as she entered the building. "Meet me at nine-forty break," she said hurriedly. "Have I got news!"

The hardest thing about school, Sherry thought, was trying to keep your mind on studies when there was excitement in the air. Judy was all lit up. Something wonderful must have happened.

Thank goodness this was a subject in which she was ahead. She doubted she'd be called upon, but if she were she wouldn't fumble too badly.

"Locker room," whispered Judy as they met in the hall. "Don't want to be caught talking to you."

Sherry laughed. This was a switch. But she thought she understood. She stayed with Catherine's crowd a moment, then excused herself.

"Sherry," Judy's eyes were shining, "Dad's all for the plan. And he thought up something even better. He has an acre where an old house burned down, family orchard 'n' everything. He's going to tell the boys if they want to pay the rent by fixing up the house so it can be moved next summer, he'll sell them the acre for it to go onto. And he'll lump the cost of the house with the acre, all on easy payments."

"You certainly got the clouds out of your branches," breathed Sherry. "But how will they buy the place when they can't pay rent now?"

"Oh, field work in the summer. They've had such a grim time this winter, I think when they all pull together to buy shelter, they won't sell and go on another show-off spree."

It was certainly worth trying. Sherry wished she

might be around to watch the Pedlar boys when Mr. Scotts talked to them.

That night she asked her mother what he was like.

"I haven't met him. I understand he is gruff and abrupt."

"Good," mused Sherry. Jerry and Ted would feel they'd a real business proposition put up to them, not charity.

"Have a nice day?" Mrs. Sadler asked.

"Um, dreamy," Sherry murmured.

She had company the next noon. Two of Catherine's friends brought their lunch. She hadn't studied, but she had had a wonderful time. Nina and Dot were fun.

Nancy and Flo joined them the next day. "I'm saving for a new formal," Nancy confessed.

"I'm not. I'm loaded," Flo commented. "I'm just afraid of missing some fun. Hey, how's for having malts on me after school?"

Catherine joined them, but she was a little late, and when they reached the shopping center a crowd was milling around.

"That gang," muttered Catherine. "Look at them throwing their weight around."

Sherry looked, and saw big boys in black leather

jackets and what looked like black leather heads.

"Who're they ragging?"

Jerry. Jerry was backed up to a wall, hands in his pockets, trying to look unconcerned.

Instinctively Sherry stepped forward. "Oh, Jer, could I talk to you a minute?"

8

These boys, she learned later, were some of The Defiants. Being defiant, they were not going to let anyone divert their persecution of one of their gang.

"Goodness—" Sherry looked up at a black form that blocked her way— "when I first looked at you I thought you were Anka. He'd move."

The black one moved, making some scathing remark. Before Sherry reached Jerry a blast sounded in the center. The gang members had mounted their motorcycles and roared off.

"Jer, about the newspaper: could we take just the Sunday edition? Mrs. Malthropp likes to cut pieces from hers, and it's like trying to read a piece of lace."

"Yeah, sure. See my friends?" he asked anxiously. "They wanted me to go along, but I've got me a date with Scotts. Business."

He nodded his head toward the diminishing roar. "We go in couples; sort of saves everyone having to have a cycle."

"Oh, a cyclist club."

"No, most of the kids have cars. Cycles cost more."

Sherry literally kicked herself into the malt shop. She was as bad as Mona.

"You got a yen for Jerry?" Nina asked when they were seated.

"She hasn't," Catherine answered for her. "She felt just like I did when I saw him backed up to the wall, with that flock of vultures ready to carry him off. She just thought faster."

"Thanks, Cathy," breathed Sherry. "Those are not high school kids, are they?"

"Some of the gang were. They caused so much trouble they were kicked out, most of them going into corrective schools.

"They don't do anything really bad. I mean if they do, they don't get caught. They're just a loud nuisance. Now what?"

Sherry smiled. "I'm beginning to understand Mona. I have a 'something should be done' feeling."

"Get rid of it," Dot advised. "Adults have tried and given up. Decent kids don't want anything to do with them."

That classified Jerry as not one of the decent kids.

"Now what?" Nancy asked her.

"Simple arithmetic. Jerry said most of the kids had cars because cycles cost more."

"You don't find cycles in junk yards. And you can't pick up parts for nothing."

Sherry almost returned that her mother had not been able to pick up parts for her older car without paying a good price; then she understood. These parts were picked up without permission.

She was still thinking of this when talk switched to the Roaring Twenties Dance to be given the next weekend.

"Think up a costume," urged Nina. "We'll think up a date for you."

Sherry discussed The Defiants with her mother that evening. "This country," she informed her, "has some of the worst kids."

"No, Sherry; kids and people are pretty much the same everywhere. The difference is that we're living in a town instead of a city. In a big city school you'd gravitate to your own kind and wouldn't meet the others.

"Take Judy, for instance. I didn't suffer exclusion because there were many wealthy men besides my father in the city. Judy's father is the only one in his particular bracket, so he's noticeable, and Judy suffers other people's jealousy."

"So what do I wear to a Roaring Twenties dance?"

"Shades of TV," sighed Mrs. Sadler. "I wouldn't know; I was still in swaddling clothes. Why not go to the library and ask for books published in the twenties? They would carry a frontispiece illustration."

They spent the rest of the evening planning work. It was rather like being assigned to classes, Sherry thought, and laughed at the idea.

"Like classes," she explained. "Wouldn't a school be in turmoil if certain classes were not held at certain hours?"

"Agreed. So we plan our work that way and have time off for fun."

Now that she was rested and feeling more secure in her job, Mrs. Sadler would take their wash to a launderette on Monday nights, while Sherry studied. Then they would break the ironing into yours and mine and ours.

Saturdays they could clean and shop. Mrs. Sadler would do the week-end cooking, Sherry prepare the evening meal work days, her mother wash the dishes.

"And when do you have fun?" Sherry asked.

She was joining the Business and Professional Women's Club. Being a specialist in her line, she was eligible. Then there would be church affairs.

The plan worked out fine on paper, but before noon the next day Sherry wondered if teachers didn't come in handy. Certainly no studying would be accomplished with kids popping in to visit every few mintues.

In one way it was like attending class. Never had she been asked so many questions.

"What I don't get," Nina said frankly, "is how your mother was hired for a job halfway across the continent when there were plenty of unemployed already here."

"That's what the teachers are trying to pound into us," Sherry replied. "First Mother took basics in book-keeping, then went with this electronics firm and learned how to handle a computer. When they sold one designed especially for mill work, they sort of sold Mother's services along with it."

"I get it." Nina relaxed. "If you care enough to prepare yourself for something special, the job comes looking for you. Swell. Then knowing Mr. Scotts wasn't the bit."

"Mums had never met him," Sherry was able to say. "She's even worried about me liking Judy. But I do. I think she's super and having a rough time. Kids here treat her as though the others would think them stuck up if they were decent to her. If they weren't stuck up inside, they'd never think that way."

"Ouch," howled Nina. "Hey, how about your Roaring Twenties dress? Any ideas?"

Judy was her last caller, and apologized for coming at that time. "I waited," she confessed. "I had to talk to you alone.

"Sherry, it worked. Dad was a brick. The boys thought the idea wonderful, but when they brought their father up he was mean. I'd hid out to listen, and I would not have blamed Dad if he'd turned and walked away."

"Mean? How?"

"Oh, he said Dad was trying to improve his own property at no cost to himself. Jerry simply writhed. He and Ted made Mr. Pedlar go up on the terrace and look down. Jerry asked his Dad if it was worth spoiling a view of the river like that for any kind of a building."

"So?"

"Dad told me he knew Jack Pedlar was being mean because he was on the defensive, so he told him to pick out an attorney and have him draw up papers. He'd pay to have it all in black and white. And so," she stopped for breath, "this morning they did. And when they called Dad in to sign, Jack Pedlar shook hands and apologized."

"And?" prompted Sherry.

"Dad ordered a load of lumber right away so the boys could go to work. The Ag teacher's going to help them."

"So thinking paid off," observed Sherry. "We should try it more often."

Judy said she had to hurry; she and her mother were going to the city for the week-end.

Sherry had a delightful week-end. Clouds gathered, but rain didn't fall until she'd driven to the library and the market with her mother, and returned.

They'd found a picture to copy. Mrs. Sadler had a sheath dress which came to Sherry's ankles. She also had bolts of fringe saved to use on drapes some day. They'd use them on the dress instead.

There was one disappointment. The Clevelands, learning the Sadlers attended the same church, telephoned and invited them to be their guests after services.

Sherry caught one glimpse of Geary, just one. Mona was so in evidence he could hardly be seen, and immediately after church he drove her off to some youth meeting affair.

"I wonder if a mother can sue a girl for alienation of a son's affections for his family," Mrs. Cleveland observed whimsically.

"No, Mother," her husband reproved her, "if I hadn't put my foot down hard, you'd have spent all of your time on committees. The boy takes after you."

"And who spends his evenings on every known civic committee in the community?" she flashed.

Sherry enjoyed visiting Geary's home. It gave her a background for dreams. It was big, comfortable and colorful.

"Typically American," her mother said as they drove home. "It's unfortunate people in other countries can't see such homes and such people as the Clevelands."

It was raining cats, dogs and polliwogs the next morning. Sherry, slipping into grey rain boots (98¢), grey raincoat (a hand me down) and a scarlet rain bonnet (on sale at 49¢), went happily into it. This time there was no car to rescue her.

Something was wrong at school. There seemed to be no laughter. Small groups gathered to talk in whispers. A police car waited in the no-parking zone.

Then, as Sherry made her way to the locker room, she saw Mr. Cartwright walking down the hall. Beside him was Jerry.

He looks as though his face and everything inside were frozen, she thought.

Judy flashed past her. In the locker room, Sherry found her tossing tears from her eyes with the very motion of her head.

"Sher, he didn't do it. I know he didn't. Not now, not after Dad—"

"Do what?" Sherry asked anxiously.

9

The locker room filled rapidly, yet Judy talked. Sherry felt she was trying to establish Jerry's innocence in front of everyone.

"Someone tried to set fire to the mill last night. Someone else saw Jerry on the road leading to the mill. But don't you see he wouldn't have been going *toward* it had he set it. And why should he?"

Leave it to Mona to supply an answer. She'd popped up from somewhere. "Natural resentment toward the property of one who he feels has robbed his family of their rights."

"What rights?" flashed Sherry, turning.

"The right of everyone to live decently. That hovel they call a house—"

But Sherry was laughing. Everyone was silenced as

her gay response rang out. "Mona," she breathed, "do investigate before you commit yourself. Come on, gang; we can show our belief in Jerry by acting like students instead of scandalmongers. I'm for him; who else?"

"All of us," they cried, and trooped out, leaving the dour Mona behind.

At the nine-forty break the halls seethed. Sherry, seeing Judy, said she understood why they had this time between classes. "Not for us; for the teachers. To give their ears a rest."

"Sherry, was Jerry in class?"

He hadn't been. But he wasn't in custody. They met him walking close to the corridor wall as though wishing he could merge into it.

"Hi, Jer," they greeted him.

He looked up, hesitated, started on, then turned back. "Judy, will you thank your father for me? They called him, and he told them they were nuts. I think he cussed a little," he went on seriously. "Anyway, they had to believe him.

"Gosh, Judy, I wouldn't do anything to hurt him."

"We know it," Judy assured him.

"So stop looking guilty," Sherry teased.

"I can't," he said miserably. "I mean stop looking.

But I didn't know. Well, be seeing you, I think."

Judy looked at Sherry, puzzled.

"I think it's a lot easier to get into a gang than to get out," Sherry remarked.

"You mean his gang, The Defiants, did this? Jerry doesn't really know, but he does know they were up to something. Then why was he the only one caught?"

"Seen; not caught. Maybe he didn't get a ride on purpose. They planned on him being there when things started popping. I think he's afraid to talk."

"Afraid?"

"He has younger brothers and sisters, hasn't he?"

"Oh, well, that kind of fear I can take. There's the buzzer. Sherry, what can I do?"

"Step on the ignition and start that gas tank producing, huh?"

It might not hurt if she tried that herself, especially where Mona was concerned.

Suddenly Sherry turned and sped back to Judy. "Hey, just thought of something about that thinking bit. Isn't it a colossal break you did your thinking and put it over before this happened? Jerry would have been stuck if you hadn't."

Judy didn't wait to say anything; she simply raced

down the hall to catch Jerry, reframing Sherry's words.

"Jer, wasn't it a break Dad got to know you before this silly deal? And you and he had a business agreement which absolutely clears you."

"Hey—" for the first time the frozen look thawed— "am I ever lucky—" he threw the last words softly as he turned to hurry on— "to have a friend like you."

The lunch room really buzzed that noon. More and more were carrying lunches; they said they were afraid they'd miss something if they didn't.

Sherry, a little disturbed, spoke to Mrs. Hanson. "Will this upset the café owners?" she asked.

"Settle them down, rather. These are the students who take up space and service for the price of a coke. No, Sherry, this is good for those concerned. They'll buy their cokes and malts after school."

Everyone talked about Jerry being accused of trying to burn the mill. They were laughing about it, all but Ted. He was quite indignant.

"Jerry and me and Mr. Scotts have got a deal. We'd be crazy to spoil it. All Jer did was carry a fan belt down the road when a guy stopped in and said a friend of his had busted the one on his car. He knew Jer had an extra. I mean Dad had."

He hadn't found the car, but he had been seen and identified. As the fire department had come from another town, he hadn't known there had been a fire until morning.

Sometimes Sherry felt she had more personal than school problems. She had to figure out Jerry's part in the affair. He'd been trying to help a friend. Well, her mother was certainly right. One was judged by the caliber of the friends one had. Jerry had better get rid of some of his.

Then she switched to Mona. Why was she always ranting about kids being "oppressed?" Sort of a complex.

I've never seen her laugh, she thought, just as Mr. Lennox said, "Sherry, if you wouldn't mind moving back to California, we might expect an answer."

And she hadn't heard the question.

He signaled her to wait after class, then kindly asked if something was bothering her.

"It's a people problem," she confessed. "I can't add one up. One particular one," she said hastily as she saw him quiver at her choice of words.

"Elucidate," he suggested.

Sherry closed her eyes a moment. "Take a student

who blames everything that goes wrong on one class of people trying to take advantage of another. Why?"

"You are not class conscious?"

"A democracy is like a school. You are classified, but you're not stuck in one class if you work and use your head. If you progress because somebody else does the work for you, you slide right back down when they quit doing it."

"This person probably believes some are born into the graduating class, or have already graduated."

Sherry shook her head. "They're not really. My mother was born lucky, but when there was no more of the help she'd taken for granted, she had to go back to the first grade, sort of, and learn how to take care of us."

"Did she mind?"

"I don't think so. She always acted as though she were glad she lived where she could get ahead with extra effort. There are not many nations where a woman can do that. I think this person riles me because I know that and she doesn't."

Lennox smiled at her. "Then she serves a purpose. She stimulates you and others to evaluate and appreciate what you have here."

Sherry went out, happy. She could even smile at

Mona, and feel sorry for Geary, whom Mona had backed against a corridor wall while she talked. Geary looked miserable. He must be a complete dope to put up with her.

"Poor Dreary," sighed Nina, as Sherry joined her friends.

"What's her campaign this time?" Nancy asked.

"Another petition. She wants the school to do something about the Pedlars. She saw Jerry and Ted walking to school, wet as seals. They're not in our school zone and have to pay extra for bus service. Can't afford it."

"Seals don't mind getting wet," mused Sherry, "but they'd mind being made to look like a good cause. Why can't they ride in with someone who lives out that way?"

"Won't. We think they're ashamed of losing their new car. My mother says that's good; they're learning a lesson their father didn't."

"I know. Mother used to spank me and tell me it was good for me. Funny thing: it was. It made me stop and think before I went tearing across a busy highway."

"Hey, how's the Roaring Twenties dress coming? I'm using jet beads, and I'll never get through. If you hear something like a hail storm at the dance, that's me losing my ornaments."

"Jet propelled?" asked Flo, and ducked.

"Sherry, how about your dress?"

She had the dress, of course, but she had no date. They told her not to mind; either she'd have one or she'd go with them. She'd have plenty of kids asking her to dance.

Sherry nodded. She didn't mind not having a date. That was the trouble with coming in so late. All of the boys she thought she might enjoy were going steady.

Sherry groaned.

"Indigestion?" asked Flo.

"Starvation," corrected Sherry. It was. The one steady date she wanted she couldn't have, ever. He was but taken.

Mona graduated in the spring. But so did he. Life certainly was complicated. Next year it would be one vast desert.

Then she laughed at herself. Hadn't she learned the hard way that one couldn't live more than a day at a time?

"What are you thinking?" asked Catherine.

"About dates. When I was a freshman I thought I'd just die if I couldn't date a certain kid. I did, and was

I ever glad when he moved away. Then when I was a soph, at another school, there was another 'until death do us part' deal. Now I can't remember the color of his eyes."

She knew she was arguing with herself, trying to make herself believe she'd meet hundreds as nice as Geary, that she'd forget even him in time.

Flo and Nina said they'd pick her up Saturday evening. Larry had already loaded his car with prospects, to Catherine's dismay. But that was Larry.

"Some of these days," she said darkly, "he's going to ask so many there won't be room for him to drive. He'll have to trot along behind his own car."

Sherry went home that afternoon at peace with the world. Avondale was quite the nicest school she'd ever attended. Imagine making friends, real friends, in such a short time; being accepted to the point where the girls would take her to the dance without a date.

Mrs. Sadler seemed unusually tired and very quiet when she came in. She barely touched her dinner, and finally Sherry, in an effort to cheer her, told her how lucky Jerry had been.

A quick movement, and Sherry awakened.

Suppose the night watchman hadn't found the fire,

the department not reached there in time to put it out before any real damage was done? Mills, with their waste, shavings, inflammables, went swiftly, leaving nothing but ashes to show they had even been in existence.

What would the Sadlers have done? Her mother would have been without work, the debt of her special training still unpaid.

A gang of defiant boys could have done this to all of the innocent employees of the mill.

10

Sherry, whose voice had wavered, now came out strong. "Like I told Judy, Mother, we were in luck."

"Mr. Scotts would not have rebuilt the mill, Sherry. He had to override the board to keep it in production during the slump in lumber. I don't know of another business any place near here which has our equipment installed."

That would mean moving from the apartment, from the town, the high school, the girls. Why, she'd never know whether or not Geary was *the* one. And her mother would have sadness always just under her smile; the fear she'd so valiantly fought would return.

"Sherry!" Mrs. Sadler turned as Sherry's laughter rang out. "What on earth—"

"Mums, remember the time we were down to our

last pot of beans and didn't have money for the gas meter to heat them? We went out to the park where we could build a fire in one of the barbecues—"

"And I spilled the beans—"

"Burned your hands, almost, and the pot dropped. It was so late in the season there was no one in the park, and you had to clean up the mess."

Sherry could see her on her knees, scraping the soil with a piece of broken bean pot, pushing the beans back toward fallen leaves the better to pick up the mess and put it into a garbage can.

She had uncovered a billfold the same tannish brown as the leaves, a billfold with twenty-five dollars in it and some change.

"I had to steal ten cents from the billfold to telephone the owner." Mrs. Sadler was laughing now.

"And that's how he found out how broke we were. You had to tell him what you'd taken."

He'd given them ten dollars and Mrs. Sadler her first job. She considered the ten dollars a loan, repaying it carefully, a dollar from each pay check.

"It was Mr. Watts who insisted I go to night school," Mrs. Sadler mused. "Actually, Sherry, that broken bean pot was the best thing that ever happened to us."

"That's not what you told me," Sherry returned. "It was what we did after the catastrophe: cleaning up, then being honest about what we found. Mums, I'll bet that's why the mill didn't burn. There wasn't any billfold for anyone to find so he could provide jobs for the workers."

"Oh, go on with your homework. I am about to heat the coffee and have a piece of pie."

Sherry went to her room. She opened a book, but there she stopped. She had some "thinking out" to do.

She'd read in the newspapers about fires. She had watched them on television, and once she had stood far from an actual burning building and thought it terribly exciting.

Not once had she thought of the people they affected, the jobs lost, the strain on owners who had to determine if their insurance would enable them to rebuild and start over.

She didn't actually know The Defiants had tried to set fire to the mill, but she believed it had been some of that gang. She didn't know why they were after Jerry, but the choice of the mill pointed to that.

Hadn't Mona immediately jumped to the conclusion Jerry had had a reason? Could resentment be called reason?

She reached for her home dictionary, one they had picked up in a second-hand store.

The term Defiants sounded big and brave, but words were funny. That was why she liked to look them up, learn their true meaning; not the common one uninformed people gave them.

Defiant meant full of defiance. Defiance was contemptuous disregard.

The Defiants disregarded everyone but themselves, were selfish and self-centered. Only stupid people believed the world was created for themselves alone.

They were unthinking because they were too lazy, mentally, to search for anything worth-while to think about.

They went strutting or roaring around, feeling like big shots, when actually they were weak and pitiful.

Sherry looked forward to seeing them again, really seeing them this time.

"This afternoon," she told herself the next morning when Mrs. Sadler gave her extra money to celebrate the fact there had been no fire.

She'd take the girls to the Malt Shop and simply pin her attention on the black-coated, leather-headed swarm.

They weren't around.

"Notice? No Defiants," Nina remarked as they entered. "Funny how they're always absent after something happens."

"Probably afraid of being blamed," suggested Flo. " 'Give a dog a bad name—' "

"Like Jerry," Catherine said. "Right away everybody thought he'd started that mill fire."

"Wasn't assembly really something?" Nancy asked.

It was. Mr. Cartwright had given quite a lecture on scandal. "Judging your fellow student," he called it.

He hadn't named names, but Sherry bet Jerry had writhed. His name had been cleared the hard way.

Just as there were no Defiants, neither was Jerry leaning against the outside of the Malt Shop.

"You won't believe this," Nina confided, "but Jer and Teddy popped into Judy's car and simply streaked west. What gives?"

Sherry thought she might offer a little information. "They're working, and there aren't too many daylight hours yet. Judy lives out their way, doesn't she?"

"Did Jer tell you?" asked a chorus, and in the next booth a very blonde girl squeezed back into the corner and awaited the answer.

"Look, y'all," Sherry drawled, "except when I sat on eggs, I have spoken to him twice: the first time to tell him we couldn't take a daily paper; the second time to tell him we could take the Sunday paper. I think he's a swell kid, but bespoken."

And Jammy relaxed. In her mind Jerry was hers. Somehow this new girl was "hep."

She was talking to her girl friends when Sherry said Judy had mentioned it; hence she didn't hear.

Unwittingly Sherry hadn't made a friend, but she had lost an enemy.

The next days were busy ones, what with school and working on the costume. The girls refused to consider it normal attire even for the twenties.

Sherry finally appealed to Mrs. Malthropp, who had been what was called adolescent, not teen-age, in the early 1920 era.

"Is this anything like what you'd have worn?" she asked anxiously, twisting to expose a side slit which showed far more than her ankle.

"Pa would have paddled it off me," Mrs. Malthropp told her. "Slits weren't put in skirts to prove you didn't go around on wheels. They were there, and not high ones like that, so's a girl could run should a mad dog take after her.

"You wait till you're my age. You'll see. It won't be the clothes you and your friends wear they'll associate with that era, but freak things."

"And kids then will think we were drips, won't they?"

However, as she had no desire to sprawl on the dance floor, she left the slit. She doubted any of the boys with whom she would dance would realize a girl could be ankle-shackled.

Sherry sewed. She also thought deeply, until one afternoon Nina asked, "What's bugging you, Sher? You act dopey. Is it the dance?"

"It's Mona," Catherine said. "She has it in for Sherry; treats her like a delinquent beyond even her power to save. You shouldn't mind, Sher."

"I don't mind what she thinks of me. I do mind what I think of her. I mean she's another human being."

"Wannabet?" slurred Flo. "If she is, why doesn't she act like one?"

"She probably thinks she does and we don't," said Nancy, and Sherry nodded.

"What is her background, family and stuff?" she

asked.

"Same as ours. Two older brothers: one married, one in college. Regular home, like ours; parents; enough money to be comfortable."

So there was nothing there to give her such a complex, a need to save what she called the "downtrodden."

"Father says," contributed Catherine, "she read a book." She waited for the jeers to quiet. "I mean just one. She took that author's opinion and used is as a launching pad."

"She's certainly been way high and far out ever since. Hey, what kind of slippers you going to wear Sat'day night?"

The subject changed, but Sherry's underlying thoughts didn't. She, who was normally even-tempered, was afraid if Mona didn't change her "oh, you poor stupid child" attitude, she'd blow up.

She could usually laugh, not at the person but at what he or she was expressing.

"Like stealing," she sought to explain to Nina. "I used to go around all puffed up because I'd die before I'd steal. Then one day I was yakking away about a girl at High, and Mother jumped me, called me a thief."

"A what?"

"She said I was stealing this girl's reputation. Then she said people could steal another's peace of mind, their good name, their time. Stolen objects could be replaced, but they couldn't replace these other things. Intangibles, she called them."

"Hey, that's a thought. But how about Mona stealing your fun?"

Sherry straightened. "Thanks. That's my fault. I don't have to let her, do I? What a dope I've been." And again her laughter rang out.

Now everything centered on the dance, her first fun time at Avondale High.

She spent hours getting ready, a good part of the time before a door mirror.

The dress was lime green. Around and around it went yard after yard of fringe sewed on diagonally. For she would have looked like a barrel ready to roll had it not been at a slant.

She hoped the stitches would hold. They were most temporary.

Mrs. Malthropp came in to pile her curls high and, after she'd bound a lime-colored bandeau low around her head, let them puff out.

"Not bad," she and Mrs. Sadler remarked.

Oh, well, who really cared? But maybe the girls would have found her a date. There was a car due any time, and there it was.

"Good evening," said her mother.

Sherry looked up. The open door revealed a young man in peg top trousers, striped blazer and a flat straw hat.

"Mind if I take you to the dance?" asked Geary Cleveland.

Sherry's mouth opened; then out came the worst thing she could have said. "How did you ever get away from Mona?" Mona had said the money expended on the dance shoud be poured "into the stomachs of the starving."

11

Mrs. Sadler cried, "Sherry!"

Geary just laughed. "It's okay," he assured her. "Sherry and I never have a chance to talk. Mona's swell, but she always comes in with some big deal I have to take care of pronto."

Sherry didn't believe Mona wouldn't appear until she was in the car. And then she waited until they'd reached the auditorium, yet no Mona appeared.

Catherine whispered to her in the dressing room, "You're safe. She's off in a chartered bus. Gear was supposed to go, but father needed him tomorrow. He heard Nina and me saying what a good sport you were to go to the dance without a partner, so he dug up some clothes Dad had used in a P.T.A. masquerade."

The Roaring Twenties dance was a roaring success.

Costumes were admired and ridiculed. When dancing began, there was a general thanksgiving that modern people were smarter in what they wore.

"Don't brag," said one elderly chaperone. "Forty years from now your grandchildren will be laughing at the extremes in dress of this day."

Sherry didn't have time to sit and count her blessings. She was a new student, and here she was already accepted by the nicest bunch in Avondale High. Above all, she was dating Geary, for once at least.

"I don't get it," Jammy, a vision in pink, whispered to a close friend. "Three weeks, and look at her. I was here months before anybody but you kids talked to me."

"I dunno; I like speaking to her. She always smiles. Makes me feel good."

"That's an act."

"No, it isn't. Mona and some of her friends smile and speak, but it's different. It's like Sherry's happy and wants me to be."

"She's not going to be happy when Mona finds out Geary brought her. B-roth-er, I want to be in on that. One thing for sure: she'd better stay away from Jer."

"Why didn't he show tonight?"

Jammy shrugged. "I don't know. He's up to something, and it'd better be good."

Geary, seeing Jammy frown at Sherry, asked, "What's she down on you for?"

"She isn't really; she just needs her windows washed."

."What?"

"When you look through windows that are all misted up with fog, things outside look crazy, out of focus."

"Good. Go on."

"Hers are misted with jealousy, so she thinks I'm out to date Jerry. We got acquainted that day I sat on the egg carton. So we speak."

They were clear around the auditorium before Geary spoke again. Then he said, "Not a bad idea, keeping our windows clean. Save us a lot of grief and worry."

"It takes doing." Sherry sighed. She was puzzled. No one could call him Dreary tonight. He seemed to be having a wonderful time, and judging from the way the others' treated him, this was his usual behavior.

Then how could Mona turn him into a drip?

The dance closed early. Geary borrowed one couple from Larry's overcrowded car; then the four cars drove to the nearest city for the really big time of the evening: chicken in the rough, with trimmings.

"I've never had such a good time," Sherry told Geary

when he walked to her door with her.

"Kind of liked it myself. We'll do a repeat one of these days."

Mrs. Sadler was reading in bed when Sherry came in. Once in her own lounging robe, she went in to give a vivacious report. Then shadows dimmed her laughter.

"What is bothering you, Sherry?"

"Gear just said we'd do it again. He didn't ask for a definite date or anything."

"Perhaps he's the impromptu type; likes to take girls by surprise."

"No." Sherry sighed. "I'm afraid he likes serious girls like Mona. I laugh too much."

"You don't laugh *at;* you laugh *with.* There is quite a difference. Please don't change."

Sherry dropped a kiss. "You're prejudiced in my favor. 'Night, and sleep late."

She couldn't waste time sleeping, she knew. She sat in a big chair by the windows, watching clouds play tag with the stars but not seeing them. She was reliving the whole evening.

No question about it now. Geary was *the* one. Why, if she lived to be a hundred she wouldn't forget the color of his eyes, or his quiet smile, or the way he danced.

And he wasn't Mona Delane's steady date!

She'd felt so sorry about what she'd said when she had first seen him at the doorway she had apologized.

"That just popped out," she had said. "I had no right to criticize your steady."

"Mona?" he'd asked. "Oh, she isn't my steady. We're sort of co-workers. She's the co and I seem to be the worker. As she says, a fellow can put a good idea across better than a girl."

And Sherry had had really to bite her lips to ask if the idea of reestablishing the cafeteria had been a *good* idea.

After she had dozed off the third time, Sherry decided she could think in bed just as easily and be a lot warmer.

Of course Mona had the last word. She waited until the whole crowd now bringing lunches had gathered around the tables. Then, lightly and brightly and with so much patronage her voice drooled, she addressed Sherry.

"Sherry, I do want to thank you for taking care of Geary Saturday night. He had so wanted to go on our trip and couldn't. I told him about you, poor little newcomer, all alone in a strange school—"

"I told him," Catherine flashed, "and when I did he said he'd supposed Sherry would have had a dozen dates, she was so pretty."

Sherry thought of some scathing remarks; then she started to laugh. She stood up, bowed and said, "I thank you. And whoever taught him to dance? Even in that iron pipe I was wearing, I didn't stumble once."

"Oh, did you see Agnes fall flat on her face?" cried Dot. "Jimmy tried to swing her out. He did, way out and down. We just roared."

And they were all off on memories of Saturday night and plans for the next dance, which would be a lot easier on them. It was to be a beatnik affair. A school rule had been suspended for the night. The girls could wear pedal pushers.

That night Mrs. Sadler asked Sherry what Judy had worn to the dance and was told she never attended the dances.

"I think because she doesn't have a steady date, and it's kind of icky sitting around looking hopeful, especially when you're pretty sure no one will ask you to dance. Other things she can attend because boys aren't so important. I mean plays and musicals and games."

"I wonder if Judy realizes she's partly to blame."

"Mother!" came the protest.

"If you can laugh away our not having money, why can't she laugh away being the daughter of the town's wealthiest man?"

"I think she's tried everything else," Sherry admitted. "She tried working in town when she was a freshman —that summer, I mean—and folks made up a petition. They told the store owner if he didn't fire her they wouldn't trade there."

"Forever why?"

"Because, they said, she was taking a job she didn't need and keeping some girl who needed the money from working. I don't think I could laugh that off."

"No, I doubt the one involved could. But if she had a good friend, that friend could poke fun at those afraid to stand up for her. Who started the petition, did you hear?"

Sherry sat up. Who had?

Sherry started to school the next morning, filled with the zeal of a private eye.

When Judy stopped to speak, then passed on, Sherry asked Catherine a quiet question. "Someone told me Judy tried to work one summer. A petition was drawn up and handed her boss. I wonder who'd be that mean. I should think there'd be plenty of summer time jobs."

"Rather," Catherine agreed. "We make more picking berries and friut, and it's lots of fun. That was just one of Mona's ideas. She succeeded so well she's been looking for petition causes ever since."

Another chance presented itself during the afternoon study break. Dot, acting as though she'd just extracted herself from Mona's clutches, hooked her arm in Sherry's.

"Dot," Sherry asked dreamily, "are Mona and Judy's folks good friends?"

Dot, a vocal member of the cheer squad, gave a growl a tiger would have envied. "They used to be," she remembered suddenly, "Hey, they were, because Mona practically lived out there the first year the big house was built. Then something happened. I think it had to do with business."

Sherry carried the next question around for days. Friday, just as classes were over, a heavy storm descended. Geary, picking up his sister to drive to the city, signaled Larry. And Sherry had a ride home and someone to answer her question.

Larry's father was editor of the local paper.

"Mr. Delane's store was heading for the bowwows. He went to Scotts for financing. Scotts said okay, but he'd have to use sense in his buying. Made Delane mad; however, he took the money. As soon as he could pay Scotts off he quit speaking."

Ah, right there was the answer to Mona's class complex.

Thoughtfully Sherry went into the house and was still thoughtful when her mother came home.

She had things pretty well worked out by then. Mr. Delane would have talked aloud at home. Parents did. Mona would have heard only her father's side. She wouldn't have been old enough to realize if the banks wouldn't finance her father, he couldn't be right in his handling of the business.

"Instead of appreciating Scotts, even when he was proven right, they resented him for having the money they needed. Crazy."

Mrs. Sadler came in, looking radiant. She grabbed Sherry by the shoulders and waltzed her around, then said, "Guess what? I have a date tomorrow night. With a man."

Sherry nodded. It had to come some day. No one as young and beautiful as her mother could just sit her life out looking after a nearly grown daughter.

"A married man," Mrs. Sadler added.

"Mother," cried Sherry.

"Oh, his wife will be along," her mother added lightly, "but she doesn't count."

"She doesn't count?"

"No, he's the mill foreman, and after dinner we'll park her comfortably in some easy chair."

And Sherry stared at her mother in utter horror.

12

"Sweetie," Mrs. Sadler tapped Sherry's chin, "you look so silly with your mouth open. But isn't it wonderful? A real ice-breaker."

"Egg-breaker," groaned Sherry. "Mother, why are you going out with a married man, and where?"

Mrs. Sadler stopped short and started to laugh. "Didn't I tell you? Oh, you poor child. We're going to the Scotts'. We are a committee representing the mill employees.

"We are going to a board meeting at the Scotts'; first dinner, then a conclave. This way, having been in-- troduced by a mill worker and representing employees, you and I can accept other invitations. The people with whom I work won't look upon me as a sacred cow."

"Where does the wife come in?" Sherry asked, still

dubious.

"Wives are always invited. It's quite a social event. They enjoy themselves while the others slave over problems affecting the mill."

Sherry sat down, digesting what her mother had told her. She was delighted. Now she and Judy could really be friends. "But, Mother, why did you tell me the way you did?"

"Because you've been going around like a zombie for days. I had to shock you back into the real world, where things aren't as distorted as you seem to be seeing them."

Sherry stared a moment, then laughter welled up. "I've been having an acute attack of Mona-itis. Mother, your daughter has been working up a cause! Another week and I might have written a petition in my mind."

"Want to tell me? After dinner, please. I'm starving, as usual."

When they were ready to talk Sherry admitted there really wasn't anything to tell. The Scotts-Delane feud had been going on for years.

"I wouldn't call it a feud. A feud takes two parties. I doubt Mr. Scotts is aware of it. Mr. Delane was proven wrong and, though he's benefiting, isn't big enough to concede this. He and his family are the ones to suffer."

"And Judy," Sherry reminded her.

"Because Judy hasn't learned to laugh at what is going on."

"You mean laugh at Mona?"

"You know I don't. Mona believes she has a cause. She's built it up to a big scarecrow and lives in its shadow. Judy knows it isn't true, but she lets it frighten her."

"I don't call being fired, in public with people asking for it, being afraid of nothing."

"Dig down to the underlying reason Judy took a job she didn't need and probably didn't want. Now scat." And Mrs. Sadler picked up the evening paper, settled back with a sigh of contentment and began to read.

Indignantly Sherry stalked to her room, turned on a wall heater but no lights, and sat staring at the rain sheeting the window.

Poor little Judy, misjudged even by Sherry's mother. Look at the way she went around. Take her car. Why, there was hardly a kid in school with a car that hadn't a better one than she. And her clothes. She looked downright dowdy.

She needn't. She was playing herself down, trying to

show the other kids she was no different from them.

"Oh, for Pete's sake," she said aloud, jumped up and went in to lay a firm hand on her mother's newspaper.

"I came to," she announced. "Judy took that job to prove she was no different from anyone else. Okay. If she hadn't felt different she wouldn't have needed to prove it."

"Slow down and back up," ordered Mrs. Sadler. "Had she not allowed others to make her feel that way—"

"I know." Sherry was eager now. "If someone told me I wore my face on top of my head instead of at the front side, I wouldn't worry and try to prove them wrong. I'd—"

The door buzzer sounded. Sherry almost skidded to answer the call.

"How's for going to the basketball game tonight?" asked Geary Cleveland. "I didn't know I'd be free until a few moments ago."

Sherry set an all-time record for dressing.

Once, during the game, she wondered if half the reason they were enjoyed it wasn't the relief of being able to yell like little kids without being considered off-beat.

She was so completely and utterly joyous no timid clapping of hands or small hoots could have expressed her feeling.

Then, during intermission, she became too quiet.

"Give," ordered Geary, who turned from talking to a friend on the other side.

Sherry nodded across the floor. "She's like a rosebush afraid to put out blossoms," she said.

Geary shook his head. "You seeing something I'm not? Oh oh, in dark green? Girl, you may have something. So what do we do to bring on the buds?"

"Sunshine?"

"Warmth. I've got it. If we can cut her out of that herd of 'Yes Judys,' what say we take her with us after the game?"

Not only was Judy willing, but when Geary had talked to Catherine, Nina and their friends, they agreed.

Judy didn't put forth any buds, but she did unfurl her branches a little. Only Sherry knew why she left early. Her father had brought her in and was driving her home. She had to get away before he left his Civic Improvement Club meeting.

"Otherwise he'll pay the bill, and you know how the

boys will feel."

"Kindergarten babes lined up at a soda fountain," agreed Sherry.

Judy frowned. "He was so poor when he was their age, he couldn't even take himself to a soda fountain."

Word travels fast among high school students. Mona was called out of bed the next morning. One of her close friends had actually heard, with her own ears, Geary Cleveland inviting Judy Scotts to go out for a feed after the game.

Mona defended him swiftly. To her he had committed the unpardonable sin—associated with a Scotts —but she didn't intend for anyone to know how she felt.

"Purely business," she flashed. "The Transient Troopers need money to rehabilitate houses for the summer fruit fleet."

"But County Welfare takes care of those," objected the friend, and paid for her remark. She was "given a talking to" until her mother, patiently waiting for the telephone, stopped the monologue.

Geary actually was busy on the rehabilitation of a cottage, the Cleveland's beach cottage. With his father he'd left for the coast at dawn.

"I trust you'll have some time this year to enjoy the fruits of your hard labor," his father remarked rather pompously. "Last year—"

"Yeah, I know. But Sherry isn't a 'poor unfortunate.' I think she and her mother would like a week-end here once in a while."

By noon Mrs. Delane was threatening to have the telephone removed. It had become a menace.

Mona, sadly lacking a sense of humor, would have told her she was mending fences with the phone, except that she didn't see it in exactly that way.

She merely knew that Geary was getting out of her control, and she intended to do something about it before he was "lost."

Without a telephone, she took her activity to the one spot in which she'd find students even on a Saturday.

With her went a meek freshman, awed at being invited for a coke by a mighty senior.

"Sure looks funny not to see Jerry leaning against the wall, doesn't it?" she asked.

"Jerry," Mona informed her in a solemn voice, "has become a different and a difficult boy since that Sherry

Sadler moved here. She's put him up to something."
Mona went on; then the door of the Malt Shop closed
on the rest.

A leather-hooded head dipped at another. "Get that?
But who's this Sherry?"

"Oh, that laughing girl. Not good. She could turn a
chicken into a rat any day."

"Yeah, maybe we'd better ejicate her."

"Aw, now look, guys, she's not dating Jerry. I asked
Jammy. Old Moanin' Low's sore because Dreary's taking her places."

"So Mona's been here right along. Jerry didn't fumble till this other dame come along. Use your head."

Sherry was using hers. She was sewing on buttons,
pressing, ironing, getting everything she owned ready
to be swiftly donned. Her mother seemed to have been
right. Geary was an "impromptu."

"Only he isn't really. It's just because he never knows
in advance when he can get out of one of Mona's
projects."

Mrs. Sadler came in so Sherry could view her before
she started out for the dinner at the Scotts'.

"I suggested I drive; then the Wendalls won't have

to come clear out of their way to bring me home."

"Oh, Mums, do you mind if I go part way with you? I need some thread for that coral-colored skirt. I can walk home; it's lovely out now."

The shopping center was busy with people stopping in for week-end shopping after work. Sherry waved her mother on and went into a variety shop.

Thread, and while she was about it some bias binding, and she could fix a skirt of her mother's.

Leaving the store, she saw the lights flash on, though the sky was still bright with afterglow. She'd better hurry, or she'd be stumbling the last two blocks in the dark.

Happily she walked along, sensing spring close at hand, marveling at it coming so early in the year. Back home there would be weeks of bad weather before the promise of fruit blossoms. Here the buds were fat.

A grinding roar shattered the quiet residential street. One, two, then three motorcycles roared past, made an illegal U turn and swept back to come to a stop just opposite her.

"Sherry," the first rider called her by name. "come on; I'm riding you home. Step on it; I mean it."

Sherry looked at the three dark figures. She thought of the equally dark apartment. Her mother wasn't there. Mrs. Malthropp didn't know she had gone out.

She wasn't moving in their direction. Three cycles were stopped, leaning at a drunken angle as their riders hopped off and came toward her.

13

Suddenly Sherry's head tipped back and her laughter rang out. Nearby a man coming out to pick up his evening paper paused and smiled. He looked over and down at the scene.

"What's funny?" demanded the first figure.

"You three. You look like the three bears."

"Don't be smart; you're going riding with me."

Sherry backed off a little. "But I don't know you. And if I did, I wouldn't in these clothes."

On the porch the man made ready, then, startled, heard a new voice and saw a small, white-haired fury advance.

"What do you kids think you're doing?" demanded the newcomer.

"You should know. Jerry's holed in down at her

place."

"If he is, he's sprouted wings in the last ten minutes. And what if he was there?"

"We want some info. You know how he's chickened out since she showed up."

It was then the smallest piped up in an aggrieved falsetto, "She said we looked like the three bears."

Jammy's laugh was harsh. "You do. That street light's behind you, baby bear. Now climb back on your bikes and shove off. You're after the wrong girl."

They wanted to argue, but Jammy hadn't time. "Come on, Sherry," she ordered, and happily Sherry obeyed, though she felt poison-dipped arrows were aimed at her back.

"Just tell us—" the largest one followed— "how come you showed up in this part o' town?"

Jammy wheeled. "Okay. I got tipped off you lame brains were after Sherry. She's a good kid. Now scram before I start yelling for the cops."

Scramming, Sherry decided, was a noisy process. Heads appeared at windows, figures at doors. But scramming obviously didn't mean they were leaving the vicinity. They provided a raucous escort.

Jammy stopped at the gate. "Do come in," Sherry

insisted. "You've been swell. Honestly, I didn't know what was happening and what to do about it."

"Well," Jammy hesitated, "maybe I'd better. No one home, is there?"

"No, Mother has a business meeting."

"Business," ridiculed Jammy. "I saw the road she turned into."

"She's a member of a committee at the mill that is meeting with the board members tonight. They're using Mr. Scotts' house."

"Oh, well."

Jammy followed her in, pausing to say, "You'd better get the habit of locking your doors. Kids here act before they think sometimes." And then she laughed at herself. "I did, didn't I, figuring your mom was out socializing."

"Cheer up. I have the all-time high rating on snap judgment."

She turned on lights, and the other girl looked around. "Boy, this must cost a mint. It's sharp."

"Nu-uh, it's the drapes and slip covers and things. We had to live in such dreary places we made them up to carry with us. Jammy, any reason you shouldn't stay and have dinner with me?"

The other girl waited a few moments, then gave a grudging, "Why not?"

"You can call your mother."

"You kidding? We can't afford a phone."

"Neither can we, but the landlady lets me use hers."

Sherry was positive Jammy missed nothing in the small apartment.

"Jer didn't say it was *this* nice," she observed.

"He was here only that one evening just after we moved in. About the paper, you know. We hadn't had time to doll the place up yet."

"Oh."

One word, but it carried a great deal of meaning.

"I kinda look after Jerry," Jammy explained eventually. "He's got such a soft head, he gets in with the wrong kind because they look impor."

Impor? Oh, important.

"I think he'd do a stretch if he figured he'd have a leather jacket when he got out. He's not mean like the others; he's just not smart. He don't get it when they use him."

Sherry let her talk. She found Jammy and Jerry had known each other over a number of years. Their parents were "fruit tramps," or had been until they'd settled in Avondale.

Jammy watched Sherry set the table and grumbled she need not go to any fuss for her.

"I'm not. Mums and I got into the bad habit of snatching food any place; then one time we went out to a nice dinner and almost forgot how to act. So we laid down a law."

"You try that with a bunch of little kids. Don't work."

"But I'd rather have the little kids," Sherry insisted. "Life can be lonesome."

And another of Jammy's defenses was lowered. Sherry, she knew, was sincere.

She was drying dishes when she began talking about "that Judy Scotts making a play for Jerry."

Jerry was older than Judy; it was just not being able to go to school regularly that had put him in a lower grade. It made her just sick to see him running for Judy's car. He'd always had too much pride to take anything from the Scotts or anyone else before.

Sherry placed the last dish on the rack and turned. "Jammy, you have it all wrong. Jer and Ted are doing something proud. I think they're afraid to tell because it's kind of too wonderful. They want to make sure of it first. They ride with Judy to save time."

"Something with lumber?" asked Jammy. And when Sherry wouldn't answer, "Okay, I had a kid drive me out by their place. I walked in behind some bushes and saw him piling fresh lumber. That it?"

Sherry's laugh rippled out. "I'd hate to try to keep anything from you."

When Jammy left Sherry asked her to come back again. Jammy waited, searching her face, then nodded. "You really mean it. Why?"

"Why not?" Sherry asked, puzzled.

"Me and my friends are transients."

"What am I?"

Jammy considered this a minute, then shook her head. "Crazy. I never thought of it that way before. Okay. And what's more, I'm keeping an eye peeled. You let me know if any of that gang bothers you. I'll whittle them down."

She would. Sherry wondered why those overgrown huskies were afraid of her.

She spent the next hours considering how the boys would have reacted had she stood up to them, told them off.

They'd have picked me up and tied me to a cycle pad,

she decided. Laughing at them had held them off for the moment.

Mrs. Sadler came home so happy Sherry didn't tell of her adventure. That would keep. And she'd see she didn't go out on lonely streets after dark again, unless she was sure someone was watching.

Now that Jammy no longer hated her, she'd better go to work on Mona. Jammy had confessed "one of the kids heard Moanin' Low say Jer had changed since Sherry had come to town." The three Defiants had also heard, and that was why they had followed her.

"What I don't understand," she confessed, "is why it's so important to them to get at Jerry, sort of disqualify him or something."

As for Mona—she stretched sleepily—maybe something would happen to change her, though she doubted that. Geary was the cause of her animosity.

Mrs. Cleveland met them after church the next day and suggested they picnic. She knew an ideal spot in the hills. They should take advantage of the weather. March would bring cold wind and rain.

They went in two cars, picking up Nina and Nancy en route, and had to admit, "even without any boys along," they had a wonderful time.

Sherry spent part of the time looking west to where a silver haze shrouded that part of the coast where Geary and his father were preparing for summer fun.

Then the two mothers settled in a sunny spot, the girls wandered off together, and Nina, in the lead, turned back. "Okay, Sher, what happened to you last night? I heard you'd been taken for a ride."

Sherry shook her head. "Not quite, thanks to Jammy. Someone told her what those three Defiants were up to, and she came racing up and really put them in their place. She was wonderful."

"Jammy?" They looked at each other, amazed. "But she hates kids like us."

"Maybe you've never given her a chance really to know you. We got along fine. I took her home to dinner with me. I like her. I like her real well."

Nina smacked her brow dramatically. "Here we go again. Sherry, you have the craziest effect upon people. First thing you know we'll be buddy-buddy with everyone at Avondale."

"Why not?" She laughed as she said it. "How are any of us really different? The outside trimmings don't count. I am a little fussy about the inside. But I'd say

Jammy was all right."

"You know anything wrong with her?" Nancy asked Catherine.

Catherine thought a moment, then shook her head. "Not really. I mean she's never been mixed up in anything. She's just has a chip on the shoulder, sort of."

"I could have had," said Sherry thoughtfully, "if you'd been stand-offish. But I sat down on half a dozen eggs, and that really launched me."

They talked a little of the Defiants, then of students who'd come in with the fruit pickers and later settled there.

Jammy, they confessed, was a good student. She'd made the honor roll in the first nine weeks.

"Maybe it's that fool hair bleach," sighed Catherine.

The "hair-do" was changed, they noticed on Monday, nor was there too much of the bleached hair remaining. Jammy appeared with the shortest haircut in school and attracted more attention than she had when she had first appeared with the bleach.

"Hair's coming out," she told Sherry when she stopped with the girls. "I guess I had too many chemicals for a head like mine to carry. Well, be seeing you."

"Wait." Nancy spoke. "Why don't you lunch with us? I'll bet between us we've got enough. Tomorrow you can bring yours."

"Please do," urged Sherry.

Jammy waited a moment, then saw her friends waiting, "Like to, but I can't let them down. Maybe tomorrow we'll all be there."

As she went out Mona came in, seeing no one but Sherry.

"You owe me an apology," she said angrily, "and if you don't make it here before everybody, I'm seeing you report to Mr. Cartwright immediately."

14

Never had silence dropped on the room so rapidly before. Where nearly a hundred students had been rattling lunch boxes, talking, laughing, crumpling paper, a sudden and complete lack of sound allowed Mona's last sentence to stand out like an electric sign in the dark.

Perhaps the most interested were three teachers seated just out of sight around the ell.

Sherry stared at Mona in amazement as she searched her immediate past to recall any insult to the angry girl facing her.

"I'm sorry," there was laughter in her voice, "but I haven't the faintest idea what I'm supposed to have done that requires an apology."

"Oh, yes, you have. You've gone all over telling

everyone I egged The Defiants into kidnapping you Saturday night."

Sherry's laughter rippled. "But I'm not kidnapped, nor was I, so how could I have said that?"

"There are people," Mona informed her darkly, "who try to call attention to themselves by dramatizing themselves."

"You can say that again," flashed Nina, and from some of the students came applause.

The three teachers exchanged glances, then decided to sit this one out. Here was a behavior problem. They would allow their charges to work it out unless they became rowdy.

Mona was talking again. "You've been here only a little over a month, and the whole school has changed. I dread to think what Avondale will be by the end of the term."

"But I haven't done anything," Sherry said in a thoughtful tone.

"You have. You've deliberately tried to undermine the rehabilitation program the serious students were carrying on for the underprivileged."

Now Sherry's laughter did ring out. "Mona, this is one swell school, full of wonderful kids. I didn't know any needed rehabilitation. As for being underprivileged, all of us have the privilege of changing anything that needs changing, if we care enough.

"If we do it ourselves as I've had to, we feel better inside. We're not scared of living any more. We've proven we can take it."

"You are deliberately getting away from the apology which I demand."

Sherry, who had stood up, sat down. "Sorry; I can't apologize for something I haven't done. You'd better go to Mr. Cartwright."

Mona made an abrupt right-about and stalked out. Normal sound resumed, though it was a little high-pitched and slightly indignant.

One senior smoothed back too long hair and scowled at his younger brother. "Keep your trap shut, huh? I don't want it breezed around I had an invite to join the gang. If they'd pick on a swell chick like Sherry, that's not for me."

"Thought you said you could get a white leather jacket."

"Lived this long without. I can work next summer and buy me a dozen."

Catherine sat wrapped in gloom. "Poor Geary," she

answered when asked why, "is he ever in a spot!"

"Yeah," the others agreed.

Catherine asked Sherry to wait for her after school. She wanted to walk home with her, alone. She had things to say.

Sherry spent the afternoon waiting for a call to the principal's office. There was no one to tell her it wouldn't be forthcoming.

News had traveled as usual. One student crammed the last of her lunch into her mouth and shot off down the street to the Malt Shop.

"I'll take the wind out of her sails," stated Jammy. And she did. She talked to the principal before Mona reached him.

Cartwright was a most unhappy man. A member of various civic organizations, he had heard businessmen discuss the gang who called themselves The Defiants.

Night lights had been shot out, thirteen in one evening. The police assumed this happened during the period when they thought they had the group under surveillance.

Ranchers accepted the theft of tools and motor parts without protest. One or two had gone to the sheriff and suffered reprisals. Family pets had been shot from the roadside, windows shattered by distant gunfire.

"Jamaica," he queried when she was through giving an accurate account of what had occurred on Saturday, "why are these boys so interested in Jerry? Are they afraid he will *rat*?"

"He doesn't know enough," Jammy protested quickly. "You have to earn your way in, and I saw he didn't. Jerry hasn't got much of a head, but he's got good hands. Like I told him, if he'd learn to use them, he'd earn more than that outfit will even see at a distance."

"Then why—"

"Oh, that. If once they mark a kid for their gang, they get sore if he doesn't come through. They don't know how much info he's picked up, and they're not letting anything out—names of members, where they meet, things like that."

"And you do know."

"Not me. Like Mom says, if you don't want to get dirty, keep away from mud puddles. But you make Mona lay off Sherry. Mona's just jealous because Geary likes her."

Later, when Mona sailed in, full of righteous indignation, she was silenced.

Instead of the assurance of a public apology from

Sherry, she received a lesson on careless talk, especially in public places.

Sherry passed Geary and Mona after school. Mona was talking earnestly, and Geary was looking miserable.

Outside, she met Catherine, who'd also watched.

"Thank goodness I know the truth," she said loyally. "Jammy right up and told everyone on her school bus this morning. She thought she was doing it for you." Sherry laughed. "That one backfired. However, I'm glad she's for me. She's so intense in her likes and dislikes."

Catherine then told her why she wanted to talk to her alone. It was about Geary. He was "hepped" on responsibility. She guessed he'd heard her mother and father talk about civic duty ever since he was old enough to sit up to the table.

"Then he found out he could get up before a crowd and talk easily. Other kids liked him. He is always being made president of something.

"That was fine until Mona took over and sold him on helping the downtrodden. He was to be their voice.

"Things have been rugged around here the last few years. You know about the thousands who've moved into the State. The Chamber of Commerce really out-did itself, advertising this as the land of opportunity.

"Well, until these families got 'adjusted,' as Dad calls it, they were in a bad way. That's when Mona began building up the 'let's help the poor unfortunates' movement. And Geary got involved."

"But, Cathy, people do need help. Mother and I did."

"I know it. It's like having a disease. Maybe you need a doctor and maybe you have a sign put on your house. But you get well. You don't have to keep on wearing a sign or being treated like maybe you were some queer kind of a two-legged animal, different from everybody else."

Sherry laughed happily. Catherine was putting her thoughts into words. But Mona would keep the "once helped" forever apart from the "helping," as though they were a different and inferior breed.

"What I mean is, don't blame Geary," Catherine ended. "He's hep; he just hasn't figured a way out with-out letting a lot of people down."

Sherry went into the house, thinking the Monas of the world surely made things difficult for others.

She was still pondering when her mother came home

and was completely unprepared for her sharp, "Sherry, why didn't you tell me about the kidnapping attempt?"

Sherry looked up to find her mother's face white, her eyes immense and darkly circled.

"I had to learn from the checker at the market."

Sherry began to laugh, and even before she spoke Mrs. Sadler removed her hat, sat down and started to relax.

"Coffee?" She'd made some fresh and early. "Here. You're the one who warns me not to listen to false talk."

"But you did go out Saturday evening while I was away."

"No, the funny little episode happened when I was on my way back from the market. Mums, it was funny. I told Papa Bear I couldn't ride on his motorcycle."

"Motorcycle? I heard there were cars there."

"We haven't enough money for a real kidnapping. And I couldn't go riding because my skirt was so long and so tight—"

When her mother had quieted down, Sherry told her exactly what had happened.

"Don't worry, Mother. Those cycles made so much noise people were looking out of their windows, and one man was on his porch, watching. If the boys had gotten really tough, I'd have run to him."

"Just the same, I don't like it," Mrs. Sadler said flatly. "You must promise not be out alone after dark."

Sherry promised. She also doubted she would have further trouble and said so, but mothers worried. She supposed that was natural, and agreed to report to Mrs. Malthropp each afternoon, the moment she came home.

"I've half a notion to call the police," said Mrs. Sadler.

"Oh, Mother, no. Besides, if they haven't heard about it, they're the only ones in town and out who haven't."

She said she wasn't afraid. Queer, she hadn't been until then. The next evening she was happy the girls insisted she stop for a coke, and included Jammy in the invitation.

"Oh oh," whispered Flo, as they turned into the center, "look what's hanging around the Malt Shop door."

"They look like a bunch of crows," Jammy said indignantly. "Here, let me up front."

Quietly the girls walked forward, and as they did so the black figures eased back, all but one.

"He's their leader," Jammy whispered. "What do you want?" she said aloud.

The black head dipped. "Want to talk to Sherry, alone," he replied.

"Oh, yeah!"

"Wait." Sherry stepped forward. "I want to hear what he has to say. You girls go on."

For a moment they stood staring at each other. The big fellow, whom she had called Anka another time, was not one of the three who had followed her.

His hair was perfectly waved. His coat was shining. But beneath the coat was a soiled shirt, and his neck was positively dirty. Oh, the poor fellow, thought Sherry, and smiled at him, he doesn't know any better.

15

"Just wanted to put you wise to somethin'," he began. "Those lugs went off half cocked on Saturday. I told them no girl who laughed like you had brains enough to frame the frap."

Frame the frap? Sherry looked wondering; then her head dipped forward and she laughed. "Whatever that is."

"Okay, so you don't know. But get this. From now on nobody bothers you, see? I'm boss and I've said. You see some cycles or maybe cars, don't get scared. They're lookin' out for you. Okay?"

Sherry made the okay with thumb and first finger and softly said, "Thank you, Anka. That's a comfort."

"All right. Just remember we don't none of us pick

on kids or half-wits. Now beat it."

She kept her face straight until she could collapse into a booth. She even managed to hush her urge to laugh.

"He was just apologizing for what happened Saturday," she murmured, eyes dancing. "As he explained, his bunch doesn't pick on kids or half-wits."

They laughed, teasing her about being a kid or a half-wit; then Jammy spoke.

"She related to him when she called him Anka the other day. Kids like those don't get many compliments."

"Goodness, you don't suppose he'll develop a—"

Jammy didn't let Nina finish. "He won't. I know him and his kind. She'll just be something special. Sort of like a kid sister. I doubt he'll even speak to her again."

Still they argued in low, worried tones.

"Look," ordered Jammy, "you don't see them bothering me, do you? They're hep to me living decent. That's it, and that's all."

Sherry glanced at Jammy, a queer little figure today, her head looking like a round dish brush with white bristles.

"Jammy," she said, "you're just super."

And the others chorused their approval.

"Just wait till this mop grows out, and I won't look so off-beat," Jammy said happily. "Crazy, but I got so tired of being treated like part of a herd I just had to do something to sort of stand out. I did. Now I'm hoping I won't come out bald-headed."

Everyone, including Jammy, wanted to walk home with Sherry, but she refused.

"It would be like telling Anka I doubted his word," she explained.

"Anka," repeated Jammy when Sherry had started off. "Maybe he is that type. Funny thing. She saw the good in him, and he reacted. Too bad he can't go all the way."

Sherry walked home feeling as though a thousand eyes were on her back. She heard motorcycles, but when she glanced back saw only one until, coming to a cross street, she saw others waiting.

"This being convoyed," she said breathlessly, running up her home steps, "is nerve-wracking. I hope it isn't a daily duty."

Mrs. Sadler relaxed further when Sherry reported the events of the afternoon. She prophesied it wouldn't last long. It was the leader's way of proving his word was good.

To Sherry she said, "Poor youngsters feel a terrible need to be noticed, to be considered important. No one has told them respect must be earned by worthwhile endeavor to be permanent."

Sherry had also been watched by a school representative. Fortunately Jammy had identified him in time and relayed the necessary information. He was on hand only to confirm Jammy's words.

Reporting back to a conference Mr. Cartwright had called with the three teachers in the lunch room, they discussed the principals.

"But conditions *have* altered since Sherry entered Avondale," Mrs. Hanson said thoughtfully. "Three times as many students are carrying their lunches, and almost no reprimands are necessary. The groups seem to merge amicably."

"Do you know why?" asked another.

"Because one pretty girl sees nothing unusual in not being able to buy her lunch and either doesn't or can't see any difference between the haves and the have nots."

"Basically," murmured Cartwright, "it is her complete sincerity. She is not putting on an act of equality."

"Economically speaking," offered Mrs. Hanson hurriedly, "where morals or deportment are concerned, she is quick to classify and discard."

"She is so completely what she is," offered one. "Those young hoodlums recognized it."

"We hope," murmured Cartwright.

Sherry didn't think too much about it. She was relieved, as the days passed, that fewer and fewer cycles were around. By the end of the week there were none. As Jammy said, "It didn't make them feel impor any more."

Besides, Sherry had more interesting things to think about. At long last she was going to week-end at the Scotts.

Next to having a definite date with Geary, there was nothing she wanted more.

She'd heard so many different reports about Mr. and Mrs. Scotts, she wanted to see for herself. She'd heard an equal number of variations on the Scotts' home, the house and grounds. Those she could take or leave; it was the people in whom she was interested.

Judy would call for her Saturday afternoon. Mrs. Sadler would join the Scotts for Sunday dinner and bring Sherry back late that day.

Sherry, who had subsisted on a few brief "hi's" from Geary, expected nothing more that week-end.

Catherine had confided in her. She had given her brother a straight account of what had happened.

"You know something?" she asked, when she was through. "Getting into gangs, good or bad, sure does cramp a fellow. Geary's in a good gang, but he's as tied up as though it were something else. Can't call his time his own."

She listed the meetings scheduled for Geary, and Sherry thought she'd just wasted her time getting ready for an impromptu date.

The other girls were a little envious. They had all been asked to the Scotts' for one thing or another: slumber parties, week-ends. birthday affairs. They hadn't gone unless there was a church affair they couldn't refuse.

"Weren't we dopes?" Nancy mourned.

Sherry wasn't sure. They'd made such a thing of it she didn't relax until they drove in to the grounds.

The house wasn't as big as her grandfather's, thank goodness. She'd always rattled around when she'd gone there to visit. It was more modern, more cozy.

The view, though, was wonderful.

"Come on," Judy urged. "I want to show you something." And she ushered Sherry down to a terrace that would provide shade in the summer. "Look down."

Sherry looked down. She would have had a beautiful view of the Avon River, but a house blocked the way, a typically mid-Victorian house with an "I am what I am" air about it.

"We lived there while this was being built. Dad planned to have it wrecked, but there were always families needing a home, and it is well built. You can see where Jer and Ted have been repairing."

"Have you been down?" Sherry asked.

Judy shook her head. "I haven't been asked."

She mentioned other reasons for their building on the flat above the river, then stopped when a shrill whistle sounded from below.

"Hey, Sherry, come on down," And Jerry came running toward the foot of the bluff.

"I'll go halfway," decided Sherry, and met him out of earshot of Judy.

"Hey, Sher, come on and look at what we've done. It's keen."

"May I come later?" Sherry asked anxiously. "I haven't met my hostess yet, but I'll just love seeing it. And, Jer, invite Judy."

"Judy? Are you kidding? Ask her to that old dump?"

Sherry's laughter rang out. "Easy, boy, easy. She used to live there."

"I don't believe it."

"Which doesn't change the fact. They built up here because once in a blue moon a big flood comes up. Besides, they like to see way out, and that house is closed in by trees, she says."

Jerry shook his head in wonder. "Who'da thought it! Well, okay, I'll ask her. But I've got to tell Mom so's she can get things spruced up."

"Don't tell your mother. Give her a chance to meet the real Judy. Now this, Jer, you'll never believe. She's just as real and human as you and I."

"Well, look, you invite her for me, huh?"

Sherry was still laughing as she reached the top of the bluff. "We're going calling later. Jerry's been dying to ask you. He just thought the place wasn't nice enough for you."

"Honestly!" came in exasperation from Judy. "Now tell me how you swung the invitation."

"Oh, I told him to watch it; you'd lived there. From now on he'll be tying the place up with satin bows if he can find enough ribbon."

Sherry found Mrs. Scotts much as her mother had been at one time: snowed under with commitments to committees and half resentful.

"I'd rather stay and play with you two," she confessed wistfully. "And oh, how I'd love to visit the Pedlars. I adored that old barn. I couldn't send down a couple of pies, could I?"

"Someone told me Mrs. Pedlar made the best corn bread north of the Mason-Dixon line," Sherry offered, and nodded at the question in Mrs. Scotts' eyes.

She did pretty well. Jerry was still worried when they met, but he hadn't warned his mother about visitors. Sherry could tell that by Mrs. Pedlar's look of alarm.

"Oh oh," Judy laughed, "that sink again? I'll never forget Mother trying to prepare Thanksgiving dinner, with Dad down on his hands and knees trying to fix it. Aren't some men dumb with their hands?"

And then she saw a new window. "Oh, Sherry, look. Mother begged for a window there. She'll be green with envy, Mrs. Pedlar."

"I do wish I had something to offer you girls, but I haven't been able to bake."

"Mrs. Scotts was dying to send some pies down with us," Sherry confided, "but she was afraid you'd think she was trying to bribe you in exchange for corn bread."

"Corn bread?"

"She's a Southerner," Judy offered, "and frustrated. Down home, she tells us, everyone was neighborly."

"Neighborly." Mrs. Pedlar sank onto the only chair not occupied with objects usually kept under the sink. "I'd forgotten. That isn't a matter of dollars and cents."

She might have said more, but a car drove in, a door was slammed, and Teddy came caroming in. "Route manager drove me home and, boy, have I got news! Oh, hi, Judy, Sherry. Open with the ears. Ready?

"The gang picked up Mona today. Nobody knows what really happened, but some kids saw her riding out of town on the big boy's cycle, hanging onto his belt like nobody's business."

"Didn't she scream for help?" Sherry asked.

"Not when they saw her. She couldn't stop talking long enough to scream."

16

There was the hush of shock; then Jerry sighed. "I dunno which to feel sorrier for, Mona or the guys she was reading off."

Anka, whose real name was plain Jack Smith, was beginning to find out.

He hadn't planned it this way at all. He had thought to put a finishing touch to his protection of Sherry by meeting Mona some day and talking cold turkey to her. Just that. No more.

"I dunno." One boy who'd gone to school with Mona was doubtful. "If I was you, I'd leave it as is."

Then on Saturday afternoon he saw her all alone, with not a soul on the street they were waking up with their noise.

Anka, alias Jack, wheeled in and cut his motor to a

putter. "Hey, Mona, want a word with you."

Mona wheeled, and opportunity stared her in the face. She'd show Avondale High School, town and Geary Cleveland that Sherry wasn't the only one to be picked up by The Defiants. What was more, she would prove to one and all that Sherry had built it up to a thing when in reality these were only poor unfortunate boys.

Before Jack realized what was happening, Mona Delane was on the pad of his cycle, had smoothed down her wide skirt, whisked on a bandana, said, "All right; now ride off to where we can be alone," and hooked her hands in his leather belt.

Smith headed for the park at the north end of town, but Mona shrieked that would never do; it was too public. In fact, she had been shrieking ever since he started.

Once he looked back. The whole herd was following. They'd held a brief debate. Jack Smith was their big man. Something told them he was going to need witnesses of this one.

"Get rid of them," screamed Mona.

Smith signaled, and the other cyclists moved in closer.

"They don't read me," he shouted to Mona with small concern for the truth.

"Circle back and lose them."

Obligingly he circled, then went off on a side hill road at her direction.

And now to the black-jacketed entourage was added something new: cyclists wearing black coats but, alas, white hats—state motor police.

Eventually they surrounded their quarry and motioned him to the curb.

"You all right?" one asked Mona.

"Certainly. We were only trying to find a private place to talk."

"She was," Smith said with an utter lack of gallantry.

"Okay, back to town. Her father has put in a complaint. Kidnapping."

Silently, at least without comment, the long line returned to town. Sullenly the black-jacketed boys filed into the juvenile courtroom.

"Daughter," Mr. Delane's voice was husky, "are you all right? Have these hoodlums—"

"Father," she checked him sharply, "I was not kidnapped."

Jack Smith wanted to talk, and the judge nodded. "She wasn't. I mean she hopped on the cycle and ordered me to ride off before I knew what'd happened. Said she wanted to talk private."

"About what? What did she say?"

Smith shrugged. "Couldn't find a place to suit her. Not that she didn't talk," he admitted, "but she didn't make sense."

The judge, who played chess with Mr. Delane, nodded. Mona was their reason for playing at his home.

"Well, Mona?"

"First he said he wanted to talk, so I grasped the opportunity. We simply must find a suitable clubhouse for these poor, unfortunate boys so they will not be forced to hang around on street corners."

"We have a clubhouse."

Mona gave him a pitying smile. "For boys of a different class."

"Well, as there is no charge, you boys run along. Quietly," he called after them.

"Wait." Mona went quickly to Smith. "You said you wanted to talk to me. What about?"

He stared at her with opaque eyes. To save himself he couldn't remember. All he wanted was out.

"There—" she turned dramatically to her audience—"I told you there was nothing to that Sherry kidnapping scare. Why, Jack would have brought me back any minute I asked."

Jack managed to reach the street before he confirmed this. "And how!" he breathed.

Sherry and Judy thought they'd die of curiosity. Jerry said they needn't worry about anything really happening to Mona.

"Look," he begged earnestly, "they're not really bad kids; they just haven't got anything to do that's fun. They have no place to go and a lot of gas to get there, so they do crazy things."

To use up the gas, the energy, thought Sherry.

"Where do they get the money to buy their motorcycles and those jackets and all the gas?" Sherry wondered aloud.

She'd touched a tender spot. Jerry wheeled with an abrupt, "I've got to get this done before dark."

At the Scotts', Sherry called Nan, who had an uncle on the police force, and Nan, alerted, promised to call back.

She was laughing when she did. "I had Mother make the call. She was willing. She was terribly upset. When

Uncle Ned told her the boys didn't kidnap Mona; she sort of kidnapped them. She wanted to talk to the 'poor unfortunates.'"

Telling Judy later, Sherry said, "That's queer. Nan said the boys aren't 'poor unfortunates,' as Mona classified them. Some come from very well to do families. But I'll bet their leader doesn't."

"I think Jerry was right," Judy commented. "They have too much gas and no place to go. And maybe they want to get there too soon."

"Which means," Sherry translated, "they don't care enough about any goal to work for it. I'm glad I have a good reason for working at school."

"Me, too. I want to get through college before I'm too old, so I can work a couple of years at least before I marry."

Sherry finally met Mr. Scotts, who spoke gruffly to her bringing twinkles to her eyes. He was like her grandfather: a big softie and trying to hide it from the rest of the world.

The whole week-end was delightful. Sherry walked with her mother and the Scotts in their garden and caught the wistful look in Mrs. Sadler's eyes and the next morning had a pre-school conference with Mrs.

Malthropp.

That evening she hurried home from school to measure the area behind their apartment.

Former tenants had used it as a drying yard, as a playground, but for little else. There were shrubs with broken branches, and there was a tree. All Sherry needed was knowledge and experience.

She considered this as she scanned the high school library shelves. Occasionally her after-school thoughtful periods were diverted by talk of Mona and The Defiants.

Mona was, mistakenly, trying to take some glory from Sherry when she told of "those wonderful boys who wouldn't harm anyone." As Sherry had never discussed her experience, Mona's story fell very flat.

Finally Sherry took her problem to Mrs. Hanson, who promptly suggested she would find what she needed in the Public Library. As the Sadlers were not property owners, she wrote a note to the librarian saying she would gladly sign Sherry's card.

That evening the other girls were busy on a pre-game cheer practice, and Jammy walked with Sherry to her destination.

Going up the stairway, they were rudely pushed by

a boy in a scarlet sweater.

"That's the first time I ever saw Jimmy go faster than a slow walk," muttered Jammy.

At the doorway she looked back. "Oh oh, a cop."

While Sherry went to the desk with her note, Jammy went to the windows, finally coming to a standstill by one overlooking the court.

Sherry, heading for the garden section, saw a black leather coat push past her, saw the figure wearing it hesitate at the doorway and go on.

She was busily leafing through books, seeking something simple enough for a beginning gardener to understand, when Jammy called her.

"Did you see that?" Jammy asked, eyes bright. "Remember Jimmy pushing past us and me seeing a cop just afterward? Well, look down there at that old black pick-up."

Sherry looked down to see the pick-up and to see the boy, now in a black leather coat, take a card from under a windshield wiper.

Another boy came up, and then they heard Jimmy laugh. "Just a bum muffler."

"Boy, was that keen!" breathed the second. "How did you do it?"

"Well, when he began looking for me I made a fast getaway. Knew he was after a red sweater, see? So I made a dive for the library. In there I switched with a guy."

"Lucky for him," breathed Jammy. "He not only had his driver's license taken away; he's on probation for driving without a license. And you wait. He'll have half the kids in High admiring him for out-thinking the police."

"American Revolution," murmured Sherry. "I mean, he's a turncoat."

"Like the early Americans who were too cowardly to stand up for what they believed in and wore coats they could turn to please both sides? Well, no fooling."

Sherry waited another moment. "Jammy, why aren't other kids afraid to trust him instead of admiring of him? Don't they know that kind will let them down to save their own skin?"

In an aisle beyond, a book slapped shut, but neither heard a voice say, "That does it."

Sherry found some books she thought would help, and the girls left.

Behind them a tall, dark-haired nineteen-year-old took off an offending red sweater, doubled it up and stuck it behind some books, then, in a soiled shirt, walked up to the desk.

"Look, is it okay if I mail these back?"

The librarian looked up, then down at the books. Here was a naturalist's first person story of his life in middle western Canada; and here a detailed guide book on birds and mammals. The third book was on survival in the wilds.

This boy, whom she recognized as one of the worst in the town, was watching her anxiously. He was, she knew, planning to run off some place.

Where did her duty lie?

17

"Jack," she sighed, "as a librarian I must say no. Oh, now wait; you're so impatient. I'm off duty at five. If you'll have dinner with me at six, I'll have duplicates of these you can have as a gift."

A crooked smile, and he turned away.

"Come back here," she rapped. "I'm not planning anything you won't enjoy. I've lived in the wilds. What would you say if I told you I could send you north to a job with enough pay to see you through next winter?"

Again he hesitated and again turned away.

"Coward!" she spat.

This time he wheeled. "You take that back."

"I will tonight at dinner. Just you and I and no one dropping in. Dare you."

He wouldn't go. Why should he? Old crone wanted

him where she could read the riot act. He knew them.

On the other hand, he needed those books. He needed to get away, alone. He was fed up with the punk kids he had around him. So he'd been sent off to a correctional institution and right in with the same kind.

There had been that one instructor who had said he'd have made a fine naturalist. He'd helped a lot; given Jack books to read, study.

Then he'd come back to the same old grind, with his uncle's wife always yakking at him, working him without pay. And with his reputation, he couldn't get a decent job.

He shivered a little when he got under way, then wheeled and headed for the edge of town.

"I'll take that." He lifted his jacket from the one who'd borrowed it. "Your sweater's in the library. Wild life section, Turncoat!"

He wouldn't go to that dame's house, no sir, not for anything. He needed every cent he'd saved for gas, food and getting started. The heck with buying a new shirt! Maybe his uncle's wife could wash both the ones he had at once. Or he could.

Jack found himself standing in front of a store window reading about drip-dry shirts. Now that was something. He could wash one out at night and be ready to wear it in the morning.

At six o'clock a well polished and definitely clean Jack Smith tiptoed up on a small front veranda.

"Come in," called the librarian. "I'm frying. Oh, and, Jack, there on the coffee table are the books."

No one in Avondale missed the leader of The Defiants for several days. The boys weren't welcome at the home he made with his uncle and wife. They tried telephoning and had the receiver slammed in their ears.

They were in no position to go to either police or probation officer. Besides, Jack had kept from getting caught at anything until his time was up. He was legally free.

The one person who had checked on all of these points sat innocently at her desk in the Public Library. Jack had made good riding time north. She'd had a call from the man out of Seattle to whom she had sent him.

Jack hadn't minded going to him. The man had had a tough time when he was young. He, too, had wanted to get out where there were "just animals who act natural, who don't lie and cheat and act like turncoats."

She had wondered what had brought him to his decision, but she hadn't asked. He'd given a peculiar reason. It wasn't what anyone had done or said; it was what someone had *been*.

She hadn't asked questions, but she had discussed books, and in a wise moment mentioned "Robin Hood," and saw his eyes flicker.

"When I was a kid," he confessed, "three or four years ago, that's what I thought I'd be. I'd get me a bunch of fellows and live in the woods and rob the rich to help the poor.

"We did, sort of. Took fruit and chickens and stuff and left them where folks who needed them got them.

"Only that doesn't work out nowadays."

"We live in a democracy where conditions are different."

"So are kids. They just played along with me for kicks. Then they got so I couldn't handle them. I was getting fed up, only I didn't know how to get out. Then—well, somebody acted like I was somebody. She laughed, but she didn't laugh at me, see?"

The librarian saw more than he realized.

"She didn't make a play for me like a lot of chicks. She was—well, different. I began wanting to live so's I could ask a girl like that for a date. Not that girl, but one like her. Knew I couldn't around here, so I figured to get out in the wilds until I was sort of cleaned off.

"Then today I heard her say something that made me hep. She didn't know I was in miles. She just talked out!

"Man, did she ever open my eyes! Old big shot me! Why, I'd been playing around with a bunch of punks who'd knife me soon's my back was turned. I'd had it."

The librarian heard that laugh Jack had mentioned within a few days. The girl she'd identified by the process of remembering who had been in the library at that time.

"These books," Sherry confided, "are wonderful. Now have you any that will show me how to garden without wrecking my spine? That yard is pure cement."

"Where do you live?" She was told. "Well, child, that section has been pounded down by feet for years. It isn't beginner's ground. Let me think."

She thought so well a load of sawdust was delivered by two men while Sherry was at school. When she returned it had been turned into the soil, leaving a fluffy bed for the plants she'd been promised.

Sherry flew to the library the next night. "I must owe you hundreds," she began.

"Not a penny. That was a thank-you from someone you helped by being yourself."

"But who else could I be?" she asked, puzzled.

"Lots of girls try being someone else and fail. You didn't. The money was left with me." Well, it was, she thought. Jack had insisted upon paying for the books. She had accepted his money to give more value to the books, and to give him more confidence in himself.

"Could I know what being myself did?"

"I think you laughed."

Sherry's head tipped back, and into the hush of that sacrosanct room rippled laughter, bringing up one dour face. But it relaxed, almost smiled and bent again to the perusal of grim facts.

"Please thank that person for thanking me. I'm fixing an out of door living room, so when Mother and I come home from work next summer, we'll have a cool pleasant place to eat and lounge."

Sherry, who hadn't been looking forward to mid-term vacation, now could hardly wait. Going daily to Avondale wasn't helping her a bit with Geary.

And time was running out. True, Geary would be going to college right in that locale and would be home every week-end. But unless she could get really acquainted before he graduated, she was carrying a lost cause around in her heart.

Aside from that, life was pretty wonderful. They had scrimped a bit and paid off the last of their indebtedness. Now there would be extra money to cozy away like a cushion, and enough to buy some canvas garden chairs.

Mrs. Malthropp had an old table they could cut down and paint to match the canvas they chose.

Sherry had her letter man's sweater and her class ring and felt she really belonged to Avondale.

It was a dreary grey day, clouds hanging so low they would start dripping at any moment.

Anxiously Sherry surveyed the young plants that had to go in before that drip got under way: white alyssum; bright blue lobelia; and salmon pink petunias. Why, she could give a party in her back yard and invite Geary.

Wearily she lifted a gloved hand to push back her hair and grimaced. She'd nearly planted herself, and when she tried to scrape the dirt away she only spread it.

Disgusted, she sat down to dig for paper handkerchiefs.

"Now you look natural," remarked Geary from the corner of the house. "Hey, you'd better stick to eggs."

"Nu-uh, these bits of mother earth wash off easier. Hi, I thought you had a meeting."

"Somebody else did. Mother sent over a wad of base plantings. From the look of that sky, I'd better get them in. Got another shovel?"

She had a shovel. She was using a trowel. And neither talked. As Geary said, she could invite him in to wash up, and they'd talk then.

It was even more fun than the basketball game. Mrs. Malthropp popped her head out of her kitchen window to call, "Just taking some muffins out of the oven. Sherry, you come and get some for you and Geary when you're through."

Hot muffins and hot tea and the rain, having started, really settled down to drench the earth.

There was the sense of satisfaction in a job accomplished. There was almost too much to talk about.

Eventually Geary got around to The Defiants.

"They used to be a nuisance, but lately they're really out of hand. Makes it tough on the rest of us kids!"

Sherry thought of "Anka" and frowned. She'd liked something she'd seen in his face; maybe his eyes, their expression. "That leader didn't seem really tough."

"You mean Smith? Oh, he's vamoosed. Two or three weeks ago he disappeared. Nancy asked her uncle, and he said he didn't know where. Someone had checked with Smith's uncle, and the old codger told them to mind their own business, Jack hadn't done anything wrong."

"That could be the trouble," Sherry mused. "I know he gave three of them the dickens for bothering me."

"Could be. Maybe they're having an internecine war to see who's big enough to be their next leader."

They were back to more personal talk when Mrs. Malthropp came in.

"Geary, someone wants you on the telephone; she says it's important. You run along; I'll give Sherry a hand here."

Sherry smiled. She was rather giving Geary a chance

to talk, alone.

He wasn't gone long. When he returned Mrs. Malthropp left.

"That was Mona calling," he announced soberly. "She gave the folks such a bad time they finally told her where I was.

"But this time," he held up crossed fingers, "nix! Mona, so help me, is planning to join The Defiants as sort of a mascot."

"Joining The Defiants?" echoed Sherry unbelievingly.

"She plans to reform them."

18

Geary looked startled as Sherry's laugh rang out.

"Sorry," she apologized. "I had a vision of a whole row of Defiants on a potter's table, and Mona busily re-forming them."

"Hey, I never thought of reforming that way. But it is; it's a making over process."

"With humans I don't think it's a job lot business," Sherry confided. "They come in different sizes, habits and shapes, and no two develop those shapes the same way. At least that's what a lecturer said."

"Go on. What else?"

"Well, suppose one had lost a leg, another an arm and another an eye. You couldn't reform them by giving all of them a new leg. This man said the best way to help was to stand by while the individual found out why he was in the shape he was in; see he could change and start working on it.

"But of course first had to come the desire to reform himself. That's probably what Mona's doing."

Unless she'd changed since he'd talked to her a few moments before, it wasn't.

Mona's idea of reform was to set forth and raise a fund; herd The Defiants into a given place, then feed them and talk to them. She would try to convince them they were outcasts, different from other kids, not through any fault of their own but because they were downtrodden by greedy, money-mad men.

"I don't think so," he ventured after a silence. "She's sold herself on the idea no one is off-beat unless they're poor. Heck, some of those Defiants have twice what I could ever hope to have."

"And it isn't their parents' attitude?" Sherry wanted an answer to this. Her own mother was so super-special no one living with her could want to be off-beat.

"I don't think so; not altogether."

He had told her what he thought when Mrs. Malthropp came in again, laughing. "Your mother wants to know if you've invited yourself for the week-end or if you still intend to go to the coast with your father."

He jumped up hurriedly, apologized, then laughed. "And me all set to get that place fixed up so you and your mother and the rest of us can have fun this summer."

Sherry floated around for two hours. She had never seen such a beautiful day. That wasn't rain out there sheeting the windows; it was quicksilver giving a shine to everything.

Geary had refused to jump to Mona's command. He had thought things through. Above all, he was planning to see *her* all summer. What more could she ask?

Jammy came in, looking like a drowned rat.

"I had to get out of the house. Mom's laying the kids out one by one. Is she ever mad!"

"Kids get restless when they can't go outside and let off steam."

"Wasn't that. Matt had picked up a beaten up little book from the Malt Shop floor. Didn't belong to anyone, so he brought it home and read it. He got so hepped up the other kids wanted in on it.

"Third time Mom called Sally and she said, 'Just a minute,' Mom grabbed the book, read a little, then blew her stack.

"She said if any of us kids picked up rotten food to eat, she could give us castor oil. If we put rotten things in our minds, the only thing she could do was to give us such wallopings we'd stop next time and see if it was fit for consumption."

Sherry laughed with her. Jammy's mother was a thin little woman who could outwork men in the field, but fiery.

"That kind of goop makes kids sick mentally," she agreed. "Geary says it's like a kind of poison that puts your viewpoint out of focus. But you weren't reading."

"No. I'm the oldest. Traveling like we did, I saw a lot. The kind of people they were reading about weren't sharp or smart; they were cheap and sort of soiled, icky."

"I know—the kind you wouldn't be caught dead inviting to your house, even though you felt awfully sorry for them—"

"—For being dumb."

Sherry saw Judy's car drive up and shivered. Judy and Jamaica were at the nodding stage, but neither one liked the other.

"Oh," said Judy when she came in, and stopped

short.

"Come on; I was just leaving."

"Please don't," Judy urged. "I have to drive to the edge of the city. Couldn't you go with me, you and Sherry? Jammy, I need to talk to you."

"About Jer?" flashed Jammy.

"Yes. I'm worried. He doesn't talk to me like he does to you two. I hardly see him, but I've heard things."

"Well, come on," cried Jammy. "What are we hanging around for?"

Jammy, being the smallest, sat between them. Sherry was confident neither of the girls knew she was present and laughed silently. Imagine these two enemies all buddy buddy over the very boy they both liked.

As Judy explained, she didn't get to talk to Jerry any more. His father had a job and a car now, and he left it where the boys could drive home, then return and pick him up.

Mrs. Pedlar and Mrs. Scotts were being neighborly. That meant each was thinking up something from her Southern girlhood the other might like and sending it over.

"Mostly I carry stuff down, if it's late. And Teddy

brings things up. Jerry never does.

"Last night Ted brought up a sweet potato pie, and was it ever good! But he looked so black I followed him out and asked what was wrong. He said nothing, so I said, 'You're worried about Jer. What's he up to?'

"At that he nearly swung on me. He said Jer wasn't up to anything and never had been, and that he was no rat, and he'd like me to keep my cotton-pickin' hands off their private business.

"I told him I only wanted to help, and he said, 'yeah, you helpers! Just keep the trap shut; that's the way to help.'

"So—" skillfully Judy avoided a vehicular argument between a truck and a private car—"I am not keeping my trap shut. What's wrong, Jammy, do you know? Can we help? He's doing such swell work on his project, I think if anything hit him now he'd just give up."

Soberly Jammy nodded. "Lots do. They just figure there's no use."

Jammy said she was sure Ted was right. Jerry had been played for a "patsy." He'd probably been given a lookout or stakeout chore. He'd thought it was something big. Then he'd found out this gang pulled their

tricks and left their stakeout to take the blame if anyone was caught.

"I think with The Defiants getting into so much
really serious trouble these days, and it must be them,
they are afraid Jerry will identify them. If they get
something on him, they figure they can keep his mouth
shut."

"What can we do?" Judy asked anxiously.

Jammy shook her head. "That's the trouble. Kids
get into these gangs easy. It's getting out that's hard.
I'll try to think up something."

She thought all of the time she and Sherry sat in
the car waiting for Judy to perform her errand. But
they had nothing to offer when Judy returned.

"But *I* feel better," Judy said. "I'm starved now.
Come on; let's eat." And when Jammy held back,
"Oh, stop treating me like one of Mona's bloated
plutocrats. I've got two dollars and thirty-eight cents,
so watch what you order."

Both Jammy and Sherry broke into laughter, Sherry
because she was so delighted at the change in Judy. An
earlier Judy would have acted "all pussyfoot," she
thought.

They had grilled cheese sandwiches and malts and

left the little café with ice cream cones, Judy wailing there should be a law against drivers eating double-deckers at the wheel.

They were nearly home when the sun managed to slice a piece from the western sky and peer through like an old crone to see the spring world had been properly watered.

"Isn't everything beautiful?" Sherry cried. "Oh, can we stop at the market a minute? I promised Mother a Sloppy Joe sandwich tonight. I just have to prove they're digestible, so she'll go to the F.F.A. feed next week."

When she came out she found the other two girls looking very serious. "Sherry, you won't mind running out to the house a minute, will you? You've plenty of time before your mother gets home."

Sherry looked at Jammy. Wonderful! Another barrier was down. "I'd love it," she said.

Later Jammy was to tell Sherry she was glad she didn't live at the Scotts'. Sure it was beautiful, but my, wasn't it lonely! She guessed homes were like shoes: you enjoyed those that fitted you best.

Nancy and Flo wheeled in soon afterward. Judy was delighted to have them drop in so informally after years of being treated like someone beyond the pale.

They were bubbling with news of a Mona mass meeting. She had planned it for the park, but the rain took care of that, and she finally settled for the City Women's Club room.

There had been quite a crowd present, but they'd not been there to cooperate with Mona. They had been there to protest a lack of action on the part of the police.

"It was a regular riot," Flo reported. "Finally all but a few die-hards and Mona walked out."

"Wonder how The Defiants took that?"

"Oh, they'd love it," Jammy assured them. "They like to feel dangerous and important."

"Why can't the police corral them?" Judy asked.

"Can't identify the ones doing the damage. The leaders are always right out in public when anything goes on, so they can prove they're not involved. They say they're like generals: they don't have to get onto the firing line."

"Jammy, how do you know so much about them?"

"Lived next door to one, and I have good ears. They tried to rope in my kid brother. I pinned him down to the attic floor by a window and made him listen to a bunch talking in the next door woodshed."

Nancy and Flo left soon afterward. Sherry was ready to ride back with them, but Judy detained her. When the sound of their car had died away, she said, "You tell her, Jammy."

"Judy and I decided what to do about Jerry," she began soberly. "I'm going down after him, and you're going to tell him what to do."

Sherry's mouth opened and closed a few times but not even laughter came out. The last thing in the world she wanted was to be mixed up with anyone connected with The Defiants. And Jerry was, somehow.

19

Judy turned swiftly and went to the house. Jammy turned the other way and went swiftly down the bluff.

Sherry just stood thinking: Why me? I don't know anything.

Why not go to a teacher, a counselor, parents, adults? Why she?

She was afraid to say anything for fear it might be wrong.

And then she burst out laughing. Just off the bluff hung a head, a round head with round eyes and a mouth so pinched together it looked round, too.

A reluctant smile touched the lips. "What's funny?" asked Jerry.

"All I can see is a head. Did it roll up by itself?"

Jerry moved up a little further. "Didn't want to get

caught talking to you—I mean you talking to me."

"Smallpox, measles, Asian flu—what have you got that's catching?"

This time the smile was a little broader. "Look, Sher. Jammy says you'll tell me how to beat this rap."

"You haven't been rapped, have you? Besides, Jer, how would I know?"

"Well, what if something like what Jammy told you happened to you. What if some guys came up to you and talked low out of the corners of their mouths. What would you do?"

Sherry's head tipped. "You know me. I'd burst out laughing. Honestly, Jer, they are funny. I saw them trying to work some kid over at the center the other day. They looked like a flock of banty roosters, jumping up and down, squeaking."

"Yeah, I know all that. But suppose they frame me?"

"If you're not in the picture, how can they hang a frame around you?"

Jerry considered this thoughtfully, and Sherry added, "I mean if you're some place else, like working on an important project. I don't know, but I don't think I'd let them sidetrack me from something I wanted more than anything else. Let that wait until you're through."

"Yeah." He tabulated on his fingers. "Laugh easy-like so they'll know you're not afraid, and tell them to hold off till you get a job done.

"You see, Sherry, now that we've caught up on paying rent and Dad's got a steady job, Mom wants to get the house moved over on our acre so's she can put in a garden. Soon's the field work starts, she'll be too busy."

"Jerry," Sherry looked anxious as he turned away, "if the Defiants try to get rough, maybe you should go to someone like Mr. Scotts."

"That's out!" he said flatly. "They'd take it out on the kids. Nope, I got into this; now I've got to get out. Be seeing you."

Jammy came up, her head literally hanging over her shoulder.

"What on earth did you do to Jerry? He was moving down the path, making faces and talking to himself. Didn't even see me."

"What kind of faces?" Sherry asked, alarmed.

"Kind of silly smiling stuff. And he was saying, 'Look, guys. Lay off, will ya, till I put this deal across?'"

Sherry laughed, and Jammy joined her. The two ran up to where Judy waited to return them to town.

Funny, thought Sherry a few days later. She'd been so anxious for mid-term vacation. Now she was just as anxious for school to start again.

At least the weatherman had wrung the clouds dry. The first morning back at Avondale the sun blazed forth so heartily, her crowd decided to lunch outside.

"Isn't this super?" someone asked.

Dreamily Sherry watched the track team erupt from the gymnasium, one by one, to go jogging the long way round to the athletic field, almost unrecognizable in their golden shirts and blue shorts.

And just inside the gym the band began to practice with short blares and thumps.

"Imagine anything that sounds that rough coming out smooth, ever."

Sherry looked around at her friends: Catherine, Nina, Nancy and Flo. And now added to these were Jammy and a shy little friend of hers, and Judy and an over-talkative friend of hers.

The latter was talking now. "And my Dad said to her Dad, 'What those kids need is a couple of fields to plough and some cows to milk. Give them enough chores and they won't be running loose evenings bothering honest folk.' "

"What did Mona say?" asked someone, just to be polite.

"She said they didn't have even homes, let alone farms, the poor things, but she was interesting them in Park Welfare. They were going to make a study of trees."

It was shortly after this that some of the fine old trees in the park were found to be badly mutilated. But no one knew when this had occurred or who had been instrumental.

Mona went around with a set white face, insisting someone was trying to undermine the rehabilitation work of The Defiants and laying the blame on them.

She was quite sure of it the night she held a closed meeting. Only the black leather jackets were admitted to a feast garnered by women who believed her policy would work.

A city commissioner gave a talk on Civic Responsibility, as planned.

That night, en route home, he found city street signs twisted, some paint splashed. Faucets had been removed and water flowed freely, inundating freshly planted gardens.

Sherry was called to the principal's office the next morning and found a triumphant Mona Delane there.

"Now ask her. I can prove my poor boys were all at the clubhouse. She knows who's been doing this. We had no trouble until she came to Avondale."

Sherry, who had not yet heard what had happened the previous night, looked perplexed.

"I don't know what she's talking about," she replied to Mr. Cartwright's question. And when he explained she shook her head.

"She works through Jerry," stated Mona. "She pretends to be friends with those Scotts, goes out there, then confers with Jerry."

Sherry couldn't help it. Her laugh tinkled gently. "Jerry's afraid to talk to me since you made that kind of a statement and some of The Defiants overheard it. You remember the day they came after me."

Dramatically Mona turned to the principal. "She's trying to prove my method's wrong and her method's right. Geary told me what she thought of my way of reforming boys."

She would have said more, but Cartwright had had enough. He excused Mona and asked Sherry to remain.

"What is your method?" he asked.

"Oh, it isn't mine. We had a lecturer at the last school I attended, and he made such good sense. I told Geary Cleveland what he'd said, and Geary agreed."

Cartwright nodded in approval as she repeated what she had told Geary; then suddenly he asked a question.

"Sherry, will you give me the names of boys mixed up with The Defiants who attend Avondale? For their sake, of course."

"I would if I knew any. The only ones I ever identified are the three who rode up on motorcycles one evening when I was going home from shopping at the center. I don't know their names, and I've never seen them here at High."

"And Jerry, of course," he added.

"Mr. Cartwright, I'm positive he isn't one, at least now." And she told of Mr. Scotts' offer and how the whole Pedlar family was working to create a permanent home.

"Mrs. Pedlar is now neighborly with Mrs. Scotts. She was telling Judy and me that Jerry wanted a white leather jacket more than anything in the world. Mrs. Scotts gave him some work to earn the money for it. When he was paid he went to town to buy it, but instead he came back with redwood planters 'so the house would look good from the road.' "

Sherry returned to class, and Cartwright stared at a notebook on his desk. He heartily wished someone would reform Mona's method of reforming. Oh, well, not quite three months and Avondale would be rid of her. Her father wouldn't be president of the PTA, making things rugged on the school board.

Sherry was showered with questions during study break. "Nothing important," she said. "Mr. Cartwright had heard I knew some of The Defiants. I don't."

But that noon she was too quiet. The skies had clouded again, and they lunched indoors.

"Sher," begged Flo, "you are in a fog. What are you thinking?"

"Oh, I was just wishing everyone was as happy as I am."

She was greeted with whoops, because she looked anything but happy.

It wasn't her business to reform anyone, but she did wish Mona would wake up and join the human race. Mona was miserable and spreading her misery.

Right now she was standing up, ready to talk to a table of defenseless lunchers.

"Do you kids realize that in ten or fifteen years it will be our age group who'll be running this country?"

"Goodbye, world," groaned Teddy.

"But it's true," Sherry said softly, as her friends hooted, "though I'd say twenty years."

"Now—" Mona pounded the table, and cups and lunch boxes rattled in protest— "is the time to start working; the time to perfect the citizens of tomorrow, the leaders."

"If you ask me," Catherine murmured, "now is the time to study and learn before we start working on something we know little about."

"Y'know," Jammy looked thoughtful, "what worries me? If we ever have a woman president, it's liable to be someone like Mona. She can out-talk anyone."

"But that office requires more than talk," objected Nina. "A gal like that couldn't win a nomination. Too many others would want to be heard and refuse support."

"Oh, let's forget about the distant future and talk about the junior play. How many have dates?"

Sherry listened wistfully as they discussed plans. She'd be included, but she always felt like a loose wheel. She might as well get used to it. She had a whole year as a senior ahead in which to rattle around.

The miracle happened at afternoon study break. With her friends, she was walking down the hall, aware of Mona talking earnestly to Geary.

Then, as they neared, Geary straightened. "Sherry," he began, moving away from Mona, "I'd like you to have lunch with me in town tomorrow. Can you make it?"

20

Could she ever!

Imagine asking her right out in public and before Mona! It was as though he were letting her, and everyone listening, know exactly how he felt about both of them.

"Whew," breathed his sister, "he's finally seen the big light."

"Meaning?" urged Nan.

"Mona has had him so tied up in projects everybody thought he was her steady date. Then she got mixed up with The Defiants, and he bucked. That gave him outside time. Now he'd made it public."

"Sherry had better look out," muttered Jammy.

"Oh, Mona never does anything but talk."

"Suppose she talked to the wrong kids, gave them

ideas?" offered Flo.

"Oh!" Jammy's eyes narrowed. Sherry had done more for her than anyone ever had. Now it was up to her to repay her debt.

That evening Sherry had a whole hour in which to dream. She wouldn't mind rattling around her senior year if she had an occasional week-end date with Geary.

And wasn't it wonderful? She hadn't tried to do anything to win him away from Mona or Mona's projects.

Something sounded overhead. A shower tiptoed across the roof, liked the texture and returned to do a tap dance.

She was laughing when her mother came in, rain coat and hood glistening. "Listen," Sherry said, "doesn't it sound like a dance?"

"If elephants dance," Mrs. Sadler agreed.

She had something on her mind, Sherry saw. She learned it was The Defiants. They had local, county and state officers trying to find them.

"Not even a weatherman could trace their line of attack. Over the week-end, resort cottages were entered, bedding and clothing piled in a heap, canned goods opened and poured over it.

"Then there was last night's mutilation of city street

signs. Last mid-week, it was farmhouses, while a grange meeting was going on. The miscreants knew which homes would be empty at the time."

"But why, Mother? What do they get out of it?"

"Oh, they're too stupid and lazy to achieve anything enduring; this gives them a sense of petty power. It isn't lasting. It is like a fever. When the fever breaks, they'll see themselves as they are—weak and silly."

Sherry looked over her wardrobe that night. She'd wear this. No; maybe this. Or was it warm enough?

Finally she walked over to a wall and solemnly knocked her head against it two or three times.

"It's all right, Mother. I was just trying to knock some sense into it. If I doll up like a plush horse tomorrow, I'll make the kids think something that's not so. So I'll go as usual."

"Whatever that is."

"Skirt, blouse and sweater. Isn't it a break for me the girls' sweaters are gold instead of blue like the boys'? Wouldn't it have been utterly horrible if Avondale's colors had been red and something? I mean with my hair?"

Sherry had quite a time paying attention to classes or study the next morning. She was too busy carrying on imaginary conversations with Geary.

A date like this made right out in public was almost like an engagement announcement. With Geary asking and she accepting before everyone, it was as if both of them were saying they were beginning to date steady.

Jammy had a date, too, but she wasn't talking about it. She even let some of the others think she had been called on the carpet.

Mr. Cartwright sighed, hoped the girl would finish before he was cheated of his lunch, then opened the door to her. After the first few words he lost all interest in food.

Geary drove Sherry to the Malt Shop. At first she was disappointed they hadn't gone to the café with the seniors, but he explained that.

"I want the kids you know to know I intend to date you steady. Some idiot farmed out the idea you were Jerry Pedlar's. Now they'll get it straight."

Sherry bit her lip. This was no place to laugh. Or didn't he know that had been Mona's idea?

At least he didn't take her to a booth in back, but to a window table for two, right where everybody could see them. And he ordered a regular lunch, with trimmings.

"I owe you a lot, Sherry," he began. "Now clam up and let me talk. I really do. No wonder the kids were calling me Dreary. I'd forgotten not just how to laugh but that there was anything to laugh about.

"If you want the truth, I was all puffed up at always being chosen to head things. I didn't stop to look into what I was heading. I was just satisfied at being top man."

Sherry wished he'd stop telling her things she already knew. She couldn't see dating anyone steady because she had a therapeutic value; that was a real Mona deal. All Geary was doing was changing treatment.

"I fell for you as hard as you fell on those eggs," he said, and she sat up, "the minute I heard you laugh. Then when Judy pulled your hat off your face, I thought: she's for me."

That was much better. From then on the hour flew past in winged seconds. Geary and she talked of future dates, of summer. He showed her pictures of their beach house and promised they'd have a wonderful time.

Not until they were back in the school parking lot did he relapse into seriousness.

"Know something, Sher? This leader bit is okay as

long as you limit it to school things you know about. It's when you try to solve outside problems even adults can't solve that you get fouled up."

Sherry now had a date for the junior play, the junior dance, the senior play, the senior dance, for everything. Had she wanted it, Geary would have driven her home for lunch. But she knew he needed that time, and she enjoyed the girls.

The sun and the rain had fought their battle, first one and then the other winning. Then came the forecast of a long, sunny period.

Judy Scotts' birthday fell within that time.

"This year," she announced, "I'm going to have one big party, a barbecue. There'll be a moon and everything. Should we have costumes, do you think?"

"With a barbecue, how about Western costumes?" asked Jammy.

"Sold," they all cried, and began planning what they'd wear.

"Do you think Jerry will come?" Judy asked.

"If he gets his house planted," Jammy replied. "Ted told me the foundations had been run and set and now they were waiting for dry weather."

"You going to invite Mona?" someone asked.

"I'm inviting all seniors."

Mona, invited, declined and promptly, with fervor in her heart, sought to show what she called "my wards" they were not forgotten. Let the Scotts have their fancy affair and spend money that should be going to boys like The Defiants. She would give them a party of their own.

The Scotts' party was to be the event of the year, not because of the lovely home but because, somehow, thumbs down was now thumbs up. They all wanted to go for the ride.

Mrs. Sadler brought out two old riding habits, one for Sherry, the other for Jammy. These, with jodhpurs, would form the base of their costumes.

Geary seemed to concentrate upon a ten gallon hat with a wide brim and was scolded. Only gamblers wore business suits in Westerns.

And Jerry Pedlar *was* going to the Scotts' party.

He'd held off at first, used the house as a reason, but now the house sat sturdily on concrete foundations. And finally he admitted the truth. He hadn't the right clothes, and there was no sense spending money on something he'd use only once.

That evening, the very evening of the party, his

father came home with the unbelievable: a white leather jacket and enough white fringe to make it look like a real buckskin.

And wonder of wonders, his name was stenciled on the inside.

"The fellows at the shop said that was being done these days," Mr. Pedlar told him proudly.

Jerry was the last to dress. Naturally Mom had to bathe the kids, and of course Dad took forever, second shaving and all. Even Ted, who hadn't reached the age of caring whether he was Western or "just plain natural," got tired of waiting.

"Oh, for Pete's sake, stop soaking and come on. I'm going."

An hour later a white-lipped Jerry made a slow way up the hill, turning before he reached the top, to scramble up by foothold on rock and root and hide in the brush.

Geary had walked Sherry away from the crowd now idling around the tables. He wanted to tell her how lovely she looked and a few other things.

He stopped by some brush from where they could look down over the river and narrow valley, seemingly filled with white froth: fruit blossoms which sent their delicate fragrance to the bluff.

But Sherry pulled away, and when Geary saw her face he wondered what was wrong.

She couldn't tell him. She had seen Jerry behind the brush. Jerry had his hair slicked back and was wearing a white shirt, but over it was an old jacket that hardly came together, the sleeves four inches shorter than his cuffs.

Now she knew why Jerry wasn't at the party.

Mr. Scotts, out to get away from the noise made as the young people moved indoors to dance, wandered near the brush.

He argued with himself a long time, then went to sit in a deep chair and indulge in memories of a time when he'd watched instead of participated. He'd have hated to have been "caught out."

And Jerry couldn't get away.

He was still there, smoking a very long, very black cigar, when a car roared in, and out stepped two uniformed officers and a man in civilian clothes.

"Oh, there you are. Scotts, we want young Jerry Pedlar. His gang has wrecked Delane's store."

"His gang?"

"He was in with them. We almost caught them.

Fact is, one of our men grabbed the kid's coat."

"Here." Mr. Delane, the civilian, held it out, indicating the stenciling. "Right here in black and white. We know he made his getaway in this direction. He's in there with that crowd.

"What's more, we want that laughing girl. She's the one who plans these things. Cost me a good thousand in damage this night."

21

In no time everyone at the party was out on the terrace. At first there had been cries of "Oh, look, a police car," and "What's up? Hey, let's go see."

But when they reached the scene they all fell silent, waiting.

"All right, Jerry." The lead officer looked at the mass of faces. "Come on. And who was that girl you said? The laughing girl? Will she step forward? Jerry, Jerry Pedlar."

Suddenly there was a rush from the other side. "You leave her alone. She doesn't know anything."

Delane and Scotts both reached for Jerry at the same time, and Scotts won, and held his arm across the boy's shoulder.

"You keep out of this," Geary whispered to Sherry, and stepped forward.

"What's going on?" he asked.

"Oh, Geary," Delane wheeled on him, "this young punk and his gang wrecked my store tonight. We found his jacket. Followed him out. He hopped out of a car just before we turned in."

"You're wrong, Mr. Delane. Jerry has been hiding in the brush there for an hour I know about."

"And I've sat here for a good three quarters of an hour trying to make up my mind to ask him out," added Scotts.

Jerry saw his coat then. "Who did that! Who did that to my new jacket? They stole it, someone did, while I was takin' a bath. Now I know what happened." He turned to the officers. "And right now I'll rat."

Another car had eased up. Several passengers got out in the shadows and moved forward.

"I doubt, Jerry—" Cartwright came forward— "that you have anything to rat about. Mr. Delane, if you and the officers will come back to town with me, we can clear up this matter."

"We're taking this kid with us."

"I shall take Jerry with me," Cartwright said firmly, "for his own protection. He is a student at my school, you'll remember. I intend to see he receives the justice he hasn't been receiving in the past."

"I'm with you," stated Mr. Scotts. "I'm fed up with this jumping to conclusions. Delane's a master at going off the deep end without looking to see if there's anything to land on. Hey, Pedlar, come on; we'll go in my car."

Perversely, the police car had sped off without Delane.

"Geary," Delane appealed to him, "you'll take me in. Mona needs you at a time like this—she and the young men she entertained this evening."

"I'll go in as a witness for Jerry. For Mona, no. Gosh, Mr. Delane, can't you see why it was your store that was wrecked?"

He told Sherry to wait at the Scotts' for him and started forward.

"I want that girl, too," Delane rasped.

"You'll have no girl," Scotts said flatly.

"Is that so?"

"That's so."

And they were off. Faces scarcely six inches from each other, they had what Sherry happily declared was a real brannigan.

Finally, when she wasn't watching, her laughter escaped. Up it rang, delighted, intoxicating, the joy of comedy relief after strain.

"Don't you see," she appealed to those near her, "they really love each other and don't know it. They're like members of the same family having it out."

The word battle had stopped.

"That the girl?" asked Delane in a new tone.

"That's the girl." Scotts' shoulders were shaking. "Maybe she has something. By golly, Mert, this is the first good argument I've enjoyed since you signed the silence pact."

"Could be, could be. Well, come on, you old goat. We've got to get to town. Where's your car?"

"Where you taught me to keep it: in the garage."

They left, and the other guests turned back to the house.

Sherry waited. The big terrace with its floodlights looked like a deserted stage. But only the first act of a comedy drama had been played.

Judy found her there. "Sher, how did you know about Dad and Mr. Delane?"

"Oh," she shrugged, "they are both businessmen. They wouldn't have bothered yakking at each other if they hadn't enjoyed it. Maybe they've thought they should be mad at each other and played it that way."

"Tell me about seeing Jerry. Why didn't you coax him on in?"

"I guess for the same reason I didn't know Geary had seen him until he spoke. And your father. Maybe we all thought he felt he wasn't dressed just right."

"I wish we could have gone in with them. I'm dying by inches to know what's going on. Wasn't Mr. Cartwright super?"

Jammy had come out. She stood looking down on river flats, misty white with blossoms, a small, secret smile curving her lips.

Ever since she had told the principal the *modus operandi,* as he called it, of the way The Defiants worked, he and some of the sheriff's posse had been awaiting just such a big affair as this.

Now they would catch them all.

"I'll bet Jer will be starved by the time he gets back," she remarked.

"Oh, of course. Jammy, would you go in with our mothers and see they fix up everything special for him? I'm supposed to be hostess."

"Jer," Judy confided as Jammy ran along the terrace

to another door, "will you think I'm awful if I confess something? About Jerry, I mean?"

Sherry laughed. "No, I think I know what. You had a Mona feeling about him. You couldn't be happy yourself while someone almost in your front yard was so miserable. Right?"

"Umhum. Oh, I still like him a lot, but somehow we never can talk together. We just stutter. Besides, I have to concentrate on college, and he's not interested."

"As Jammy says, he has wonderful hands; he'll go into something requiring manual dexterity and no talk."

Reluctantly the guests left. Some thought they might learn what was going on sooner in town. Others merely looked at the time.

Soon only the Pedlars, Sherry and Jammy were left; this being a work night, Mrs. Sadler had not come.

They looked over Judy's gifts. She had made it known the only gifts acceptable would be personally hand-sketched scenes or figures of the Wild West, unframed, and that she preferred them humorous. They were, some unintentionally.

And then when their eyes were really heavy, head-lights flashed across the terrace; two cars were returning.

Jerry came in, looking spiritually battered but proud. One of the informants had cleared him completely.

"Jerry," he'd said, "was too dumb to trust; wouldn'ta listened to us if we hadn't promised him he'd get a jacket out of one of our deals last winter. But we had to watch him. He knew some of us. We thought if we got something on him he'd be forced to play."

Jerry's face was shining. "First time I ever knew it paid to be dumb. I just can't dig it. I mean I don't have to be scared about the kids hurting my family or Jammy or Sherry or Judy."

They sent him on to the kitchen, where Jammy waited with enough food for a football team, then turned to see a tearful Mona being pushed in by her father.

"Never," she exclaimed dramatically, "never in my whole life will I help anyone again. They came and ate the food I'd collected and laughed at me behind my back. They used me, used the meetings I was holding for their schemes. Never—"

Mr. Delane sighed and sat down. "I wish I could count on that, Mona. One lesson it taught you. Those boys were poor unfortunates, but not in the way you meant. Some were from fine homes. But they craved a highly advertised type of excitement.

"It looks good on a screen, maybe, if you're so inclined, or in a book. In life there are bitter and boring aftermaths. And you come out soiled. After that it's up to you to reform your life. Hard to do in your own locality."

He reported all of The Defiants were in custody except for a few miserable youngsters who'd been staked as lookouts and were not really aware of what was going on. Geary was taking them home.

Those who had been picked up had been ready to turn on the black-jacketed boys who had planned the thefts, the nuisances, the destruction. They disposed of stolen goods, and no one knew what they received. The ones doing the work got a small percentage.

He had something else to say. Jammy, listening at a doorway, ran back to pull Jerry in, sandwich and all.

"The town's giving Sotts a bad time. I'm one of the worst offenders because I knew the truth.

"Do you kids realize there wouldn't be an Avondale if it wasn't for this old die-hard here? Take his payroll away, and where would the merchants be? Take away the various businesses in which he's silently interested, and where would anyone be?

"We've resented his success when we should have gone down on our knees to thank him for hanging on when he could have cut out.

"Well, things are going to be different from now on, even if I have to hog-tie him to keep me from taking that corner I don't want."

"Now look," Scotts began, "you know women. They shop where they can park, and if you're so doggoned blind and stubborn—"

Again a laugh rang out. Sheepishly they looked at each other.

"If we can keep her around to laugh us out of our foolishness, we'll make it."

They started toward Scotts' study; then Delane turned back. "You kids might spread what I've been telling you. And you might let on it wasn't my idea.

"Some of The Defiants began wailing to the officials. Said they were having a tough time. Scotts had everything and they nothing.

"Just about then Geary took over. Can that boy talk! By the time he was through, even the policemen knew that with no town they'd have no jobs."

Geary came in as they finished. He settled down wearily, then smiled at Sherry, and she looked around.

They were all there—Geary, Mona, Judy and Jerry. Jammy had been at the super market that first afternoon, but she hadn't seen her.

Quickly she switched her mind. "Geary, what will happen to The Defiants?"

"Advanced correctional school for the two oldest; the others either go into the first or are given probation. It will depend upon the individual and his past record and attitude.

"As for the rest, I think they'll be so glad to be out from under the threat they'll watch their associates from now on."

Jerry disappeared, was gone a few moments, then returned, carrying a box of sorts.

Carefully he placed it at the doorway to the terrace.

"Come on, Sherry. You did so well when you landed on that first egg box—"

"Really, Jerry," Mona reproved him.

"Well, she did. Somehow we all had our shells cracked. Look at the difference in us. You've moved off that cloud you were always floating around on, looking down at us poor mortals.

"Jammy's in with all of you as she should be.

"Judy doesn't look whipped any more.

"And take me, downright proud of the home Judy said Sherry made her think of making possible.

"As for Geary, he's quit chasing mirages. From now on I'll bet he doesn't go all out for a cause until he's studied it."

Others contributed. The students were carrying decent lunches and had pin money to spend for other things.

"Oh, now look," cried Sherry, jumping up. "I've never done anything to bring any of these things about. I—"

"You just laughed," said Scotts from the doorway.

"And made us see how foolish we were to be tilting at windmills."

"Oh." Sherry sat down, this time in a chair, and a most peculiar expression crossed her face.

"What's the matter, Sher," they asked anxiously.

"I think—" she was beginning to laugh— "in fact, I'm sure I just sat down on Jerry's sandwich, the one he dropped when he was waving his arms."

"Sliced tomato and onion and barbecue sauce. Oh, Sherry," wailed Jammy, "I'll get a towel."

"I'll take care of her. Come on, Sherry," said Judy.

"No." Geary stood up. "You had her last time, and

look at the weeks of laughter I missed."

Scotts turned back to his study.

"Mona," observed Delane heavily, "says that girl has no sense of responsibility. She laughs at everything."

"No!" Scotts' voice was firm. "I had the Sadlers investigated pretty thoroughly before Mrs. Sadler was hired. Actually, they have been through hardships that would have discouraged and destroyed most people.

"They leared to evaluate; to laugh off the unimportant; to dig in and work on the important things.

"Look at the time we've wasted carrying on a silly feud. Our basic differences were so feeble that girl's laugh uncovered them, then destroyed them."

After a moment Delane nodded. "Mona used time and money and energy to bring about a leveling of class barriers that girl leveled with laughter.

"What we need are more laughing girls."

Geary Cleveland didn't think so. Sherry, now in a dress of Judy's, sat happily in his car. And he intended to keep her there, maybe for the rest of their life. Off and on, of course.

"You can come up to the campus for the big games," he began. "Then next year of course you'll be attending college and—" He broke off. "Now why are you laughing?"

"Because we're such foolish beings. We waste wonderful hours trying to live the years ahead and miss all of the beauty and fun around us every day."

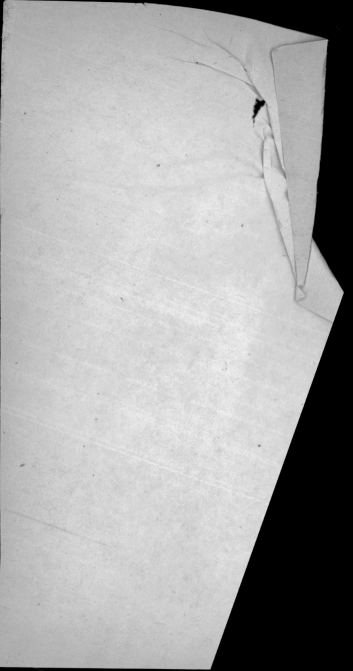